blokes down under

AN AUSSIE MM NOVELLA COLLECTION

LOUISA MASTERS

contents

after the blaze

after the blaze

Friendship can be everything... until it's not enough.

Charlie Madden left his city life behind to help his great-aunt run a quilting shop in rural Lakes Entrance. He loves his quieter new life... almost as much as he loves Archie Tucker.

Archie, his closest friend in town and everybody's favourite person, has no idea how Charlie feels, and Charlie's not willing to risk their friendship by making a move. He can be content to love from afar as long as Archie's still in his life.

But then bushfires sweep the region, and CFA volunteer Archie is called out to battle the blaze... and as Gippsland burns, Charlie realizes that some things are worth the risk.

one

DECEMBER 31, 2019

HAVE you ever felt completely and utterly helpless? Not for yourself—for someone else. Forced to stand by and watch them suffer, unable to do anything to help?

I never have before, but this summer seems to be all about helplessly wringing my hands while others suffer.

"I'm sorry, honey," I croon, patting the little girl's back as she sobs against my neck. "I'm so sorry." Three feet away, her harried and exhausted mother shoots me a grateful look as she tries to calm her screaming infant. He doesn't want to be calmed, of course—he's tired, his routine is shot to hell, the air is hot and smoky, and nothing around him is familiar. It's noisy and crowded here at the evacuation centre; not exactly conducive to him taking a nap.

Maisy, the toddler in my arms, mumbles something about her "pretty princess bed," and even though I know the loss of a bed is nothing compared to whole towns and lives, my heart breaks for her. She's not quite three. That bed mattered to her; more, it's symbolic of everything else that's gone.

Finally, her sobs peter out, and a little while later, she goes slack and heavy. I wait a few minutes, then carefully lay her on the camping mattress in the back of her mother's SUV. Theirs isn't the only car parked here at the reserve and doubling as a home. The place is packed full—last I heard, evacuees were being sent on to Bairnsdale because there just isn't room for so many people. Not exactly a great way to spend New Year's Eve.

"Thank you, Charlie," Emma, the overworked mother, whispers. Her son has finally stopped screaming, and I really hope for all their sakes that they manage a decent nap. Or at least some quiet time.

"No problem. Can I get you anything, or do anything else?"

She shakes her head. "Just... if you hear anything about my husband?"

"Of course," I assure her. "I'll be here for a few more hours, and I'll let you know if any news comes." Her husband is a volunteer firefighter for the CFA, and he's been busy the past few days—well, weeks, really. There's a very good chance he doesn't know yet that she and the kids are here and their house is ashes. Emma got out of Buchan only an hour before the fires swept through. Happy New Year, right? She's left messages on his phone and with the relevant authorities, but the firefighters are overworked right now.

Desperately so.

I make myself smile at her and then move on. I'm not here at the Lakes Entrance evacuation centre in any official capacity. There are a bunch of us locals who just come when we can to help out in any way we're needed. The "official" volunteers know what they're doing, so we make ourselves available when they need extra hands and try to help the evacuees with anything they might need the rest of the time—like rocking fractious children. It's not much, but it's better than sitting at home watching East Gippsland burn around me and wondering how Archie is.

If he's okay.

I'm getting ahead of myself. My name is Charlie Madden. I'm twenty-six years old, blond hair, brown eyes, and I live in the coastal town of Lakes Entrance, Victoria, with my elderly great-aunt. I used to be a city boy, but when Aunt Hannah broke her leg three years ago, right when my job was downsized, I came out to look after her quilting and haberdashery shop... and just never went back. I've always been into crafts, and it turns out quilting is something I'm particularly good at—along with other sewing. I made a decent amount of change last year making wedding dresses for local brides. It's a great little side business. So now I manage the business, and Aunt Hannah reigns over the shop with her expertise and gossip and teaches everyone fancy stitches in the quilting classes we offer.

Until a year ago, I was living with her in her cosy two-bedroom cottage, but we finally decided that since I wasn't leaving, we should make more permanent arrangements, and I found a tiny one-bedroom unit not far from the shop. It's not much, but I love it.

My life here is comfortable and ordered and calm. It's a small town, population right around five thousand, but because it's a tourist destination, there's a decent range of shops and restaurants—and in the summer, the population surges to over twenty thousand as all the city people come to visit. This year, the population bump is due to bushfire evacuees from nearby towns, not tourists, and many local businesses are already struggling.

Do I miss the benefits city living has for a young gay man? Yes. No doubt there. The year-round gay community here is much smaller, and worse, everyone knows everyone else *and* their business. It's a lot harder to keep anything private.

For example, everyone who frequents the shop knows about my adoration of Archie Tucker, and believe me, I never told anyone. They just *know*.

Who is Archie? Archie is... perfect. (Cue besotted sigh.) Well, he's not actually perfect, but he comes damn close. He's a scion of one of the wealthier families in the area. The Tuckers own a five-star resort, function centre, and golf club just out of town, and it's not uncommon to see helicopters whirring over town, ferrying the elite from Melbourne. It's *that* kind of five-star resort, not one of the ones ordinary people splash out on for a special weekend away. There are no prices listed on their website—I checked once, right after I moved here. For a friend. Well, okay, it was because I was trying to come up with ways to accidentally-on-purpose run into Archie, and I thought staying at the resort might do it. Needless to say, I gave up on that idea *fast*.

But it's not Archie's family or money that enthrals me. It's *him*. I met him my first week in town, when he brought his grandmother to the shop to buy fabric, and I've seen him every week since then, because he brings his grandmother in *every week*. That's the kind of guy Archie is—he drives his elderly grandmother to a quilting store and waits patiently for an hour, reading a magazine or messing with his phone or (most often) talking to me while she gossips with Aunt Hannah and their friends and selects fabric. Which he then cheerfully carries out to the car.

He's gorgeous, with curly black hair and grey eyes, a

profile that could grace a statue, and a full, smiling mouth. Seriously. He smiles a lot. He's a year younger than me and works as assistant general manager of the resort—he's being groomed to take over one day, since he's the only one of his siblings who's interested. He plays on the Lakes Entrance footy team in winter, the cricket team in summer, and he's heavily into sailing. He helps out with the youth group, organized a fortnightly karaoke night at the pub, and always has time for any community event that needs volunteers.

And he's a CFA volunteer firefighter.

Daunting, yeah? One of those people you admire from afar but who's destined to end up with someone equally daunting and impressive.

So I'm sure you can imagine how my first meeting with him went. It was before I even knew all that stuff about him —he was just the hot guy who came into the shop with an old lady.

And my jaw dropped.

In fact, I was so busy staring at him that I missed what his grandmother said and earned myself a rap across the knuckles from her fan.

Because she's the kind of old lady who carries a fan.

"Young man, I asked who you are." The imperious note in her voice could not be denied.

I dragged my gaze away from the Adonis hovering a few feet behind her and said, "Uh... Charlie. I'm Charlie."

She raised a single eyebrow, which made me instantly envious, because no matter how much I practice, I can*not* do that. "Hannah's nephew?"

That got my attention. Aunt Hannah had talked about me? Why? I'm just one of a dozen great-nieces and - nephews.

"Yes, ma'am. I'm here to help until she can get around better." I didn't bother to explain that she'd been injured—I learned within my first hour there that everyone already knew.

She looked down her nose at me, which was a neat trick. I'm short for a man, but she's still about four inches shorter. Her gaze lingered on my face, then drifted down to my hands, and I knew she was taking in the eyeliner and nail polish. That made me nervous. Aunt Hannah had assured me the town was fairly open-minded, but still.... "Do you know anything about quilting?"

"Grandma," Archie chided, but she shushed him.

"Probably not as much as you," I told her honestly. "But Aunt Hannah's been teaching me since I was a kid, so I'm not totally ignorant." I was actually a better-than-decent quilter even then, but I didn't want to brag.

The way she studied me made me feel like I might have failed at life, but just when I was ready to burst into tears or apologise for even existing, she nodded. "I'm Amelia Tucker. Your aunt is a dear friend of mine. Is she able to have visitors?"

"She's still at the hospital in Bairnsdale, but if you're headed over there, I'm sure she'd love to see you. We expect she'll be able to come home next week sometime."

She looked over her shoulder at the young god, who smiled.

"We can go when you're finished here, if you like," he offered, and part of me went from lust to love right then.

"Thank you." She turned back to me. "This is my grandson Archie. Talk to him while I find what I want."

"Ah... can I help y—" I stopped when she levelled a "please don't waste my time" look at me. "Let me know if you need help finding anything," I finished weakly.

Archie chuckled and came up to lean on the counter, looking affectionately after his grandmother as she wandered into the stacks of quilting fabric. When he turned his warm gaze on me, I almost swallowed my tongue.

"Archie Tucker." He offered his hand. Fortunately, shaking hands is a reflex action, so I found myself following social protocol without having to think.

"Charlie Madden. Hah, we both got saddled with old-fashioned names."

Yes. I said that. To a guy I'd just met.

My cheeks went hot, and I began to stammer an apology, but he waved a hand dismissively and grinned... and that was when I saw his dimples.

That's right. He has dimples. Are you beginning to understand my adoration?

"I'm named after my grandfather... and *his* grandfather. You?"

"My grandfather," I agreed. "Not sure about his grandfather."

"It could be worse," he commiserated. "We could be named after our grand*mothers*."

I laughed, and he laughed, and that was the first time I met Archie Tucker.

When Aunt Hannah came home five days later, I'd barely settled her in her armchair with a cup of tea before she turned her sharp gaze on me and said, "I hear you met Archie Tucker."

I blushed just thinking about him. "He came in with his grandmother on Saturday," I said, even though she obviously knew.

"He's a nice boy."

"He seemed very nice," I agreed, praying my cheeks wouldn't get any hotter.

"He'd be a good friend for you. He knows what it's like to be gay in a small community."

I knocked over her mug and tea splashed over the side table and onto the floor.

"Shit! Sorry, Aunt Hannah. Let me get a tea towel." And I escaped to the kitchen, where I breathed deeply for a few moments and tried not to get too excited about the fact that Archie is gay.

The thing is, my gaydar is absolutely worthless. I've never been able to tell if someone is gay or not unless they actually come out and tell me—no pun intended. I've even been flirted with and not realised it until it was pointed out in short, no-nonsense sentences. So there was no way for me to guess that Archie is gay. I've always considered my lack of gaydar somewhat unfair, since people take one look at me and just assume I *am* gay. I guess I have a vibe.

So over the past three years, Archie and I have been friends. He's a friendly guy. I see him every week at the shop, and he often calls and invites me to join him and his friends at the pub, or to watch whatever sporting match is being played. I've even gotten somewhat involved as a volunteer for the local footy and cricket clubs because of him.

But he's never shown any *interest*. And there's no way I'll throw away our friendship by asking for more—he's too important to me. I just adore him from afar and enjoy his friendship.

And try not to let the Matchmaking Quilters Association embarrass me.

It's not really an association, of course. I just made that up. I'm talking about the women who visit the shop. It worries me a lot how easily they all guessed about my adoration. Am I so obvious? Does Archie know too? Is he just too nice to say anything about it?

I can't think about that for too long or I'll drive myself nuts.

Anyway, the MQA women are determined that I'll have a happily ever after with Archie. I deserve it, they tell me, and he needs a nice boy like me. We complement each other. Even his grandmother is part of the MQA—and didn't I almost have a heart attack when she called me over one Saturday and quietly suggested I should ask him out. Thank fuck he didn't hear her. I managed to get her to swear that she would never mention it to him, in return for which I would put aside anything new that had the raspberry colour she's been working with so she could have first refusal. I got scolded when Aunt Hannah found out, but so far, she's let me keep to it.

So while the MQA doesn't overtly interfere, there's been a lot of behind-the-scenes manipulation. I can't tell you how many times I've gotten a call to please come over and change a light bulb or fetch something that's been stored on a high shelf (I may be short, but I can use a ladder without fear of a broken hip), only to arrive and find that Archie's been called out for the same reason, with the MQA matron muttering about how she's so forgetful, she must have asked us both, and why don't we go have something to eat together when we leave?

Archie knows what they're up to, of course. He smiles at them knowingly, then rolls his eyes once they turn their backs, and we go to the pub for a meal and have a great time and never talk about it. I guess he figures the ladies are just matchmaking us because we're both gay? Regardless, I haven't been publicly humiliated by the whole thing... *yet*.

two

NINE O'CLOCK IS LOOMING by the time I finally head home. I'm tired, hot, and hungry. It's New Year's Eve, but the town is eerily quiet—not many people feel like celebrating with most of Gippsland burning. I know I don't, which is why I'm going home to be alone. There's not a lot of food in my house, since I haven't been home much in the past few days, but I'll cobble some sort of dinner together and then watch TV in my boxers for a while before I fall asleep on the couch and wake up with a sore back an hour later. I haven't slept well lately. We're not in direct danger from fires here in Lakes Entrance (although bushfires aren't exactly predictable, so who knows), but the pervasive fear in the area isn't exactly conducive to rest.

Oh, fuck it. The truth is, I've been too worried about Archie to sleep properly. I know he's been called out several times since November, but the last time I spoke with him was at Christmas, and things have taken a drastic turn for the worse since then. I heard that all volunteers have been called out and are working ridiculous shifts to try to stay ahead of these fires. For all I know, he's been out there for the past week. I've sent a few texts to let him know I'm thinking of him, but it really doesn't surprise me not to hear back—he'll be either actively fighting fires or resting to go back out. I'd know if something had happened to him —and no, not because of a cosmic connection. If something had happened to Archie Tucker, the whole town would be talking about it.

I park in the spot allocated to me and turn toward my unit. It's not quite dark yet, but the twilight gloom is thickening—and the smoke haze doesn't help. It's actually not as bad as it could be, because of the sea breezes. I hate to think how some of the towns further inland are doing.

Something moves on my tiny front porch, and I stop dead. Is someone there? Who would be there? Fuck, I should have fixed the sensor light.

I edge closer, trying to see who—or what, because wildlife. We've been getting a lot of animals in town, what with the fires—it could be without getting so close I cut off my chances of escaping an axe murderer. (What? It could happen.) I widen my eyes as far as I can...

"Archie?" Shock is apparent in my voice, and Archie moves a little further out of the shadows.

Even in the poor light, he looks wrecked. I hurry up onto the porch and grab him into a hug before I can think better of it. Even though ours isn't really a hugging friendship, he holds on tight, burying his face against my hair. He smells like soap, with a whiff of smoke under that, and I want to cry, I'm so glad to have him here.

"Charlie...."

His whisper cuts through the confusion and relief in my brain. I step back.

"Come inside. What are you doing here?" I fumble with my keys, almost dropping them twice before I manage to get the door open. He just watches, his eyes a little glazed. "Have you slept?" I demand, ushering him inside.

He shakes his head. "Twelve hours off" is all he says.

And he came here. I try not to think about what that might mean.

"Sit." I push him toward the couch. "I'm going to get you something to eat. Have you eaten?"

"Yes. I think. Hours ago." He sinks down on the couch and looks around. He's only been here a few times, and only to meet up before we go out, not to just hang out. I'm not sure how much he's really taking in, though.

I round the counter the separates the kitchen from the living room and open the fridge. Just as I suspected, it's all but bare. A quick hunt through the cupboards nets me some cans of soup and half a loaf of bread. Soup and toast it is, and once Archie falls asleep—because no way am I letting him drive all the way out to his house at the resort when he's *this* exhausted—I'll run next door and beg my neighbour for some eggs or something so he can have a proper breakfast before he has to go back.

Although...

"Archie, have you called your family?"

He looks at me blankly. I try again.

"When was the last time you spoke to your family?"

He shakes his head as though to clear it. "Uh... yesterday, maybe. Or the day before? I had six hours off and I called them while I was eating. It must have been the day before yesterday."

They're probably worried sick. "You should call them. Do you have your phone?"

He nods. Then he blinks. Blinks again, for a little longer. His eyes drift shut.

Okay then.

I could go through his pockets and find his phone, but… that's a bit skeezy, right? Also, what if he locks it like most people do?

I put the soup on to heat and pull out my phone to call Aunt Hannah.

"Hello?"

"It's me. Um, do you have Mrs Tucker's phone number?"

Silence.

"Is everything okay, Charlie?" She sounds worried, and I rush to reassure her.

"Yes, it's all fine. Archie's here, and I thought his family might like to know he's okay, but he's fallen asleep. Could you maybe call her?"

"You should call her. Here, I'll give you the number. That poor boy must be exhausted." She recites a landline number, and I scramble to find a pen and write it down. "Call her now so she can get a decent sleep tonight."

"I will," I promise. "I'll see you tomorrow." We trade goodbyes and I end the call, then stare at the piece of paper. Aunt Hannah didn't seem surprised that Archie is here, but I'm sure Mrs Tucker will be.

But she'll also be worried about her grandson, and she's an old lady who, though scary sometimes, has always been kind to me.

I dial the number. It rings twice before it's answered.

"Hello?"

I would recognize that voice anywhere.

"Mrs Tucker, it's Charlie Madden. From the shop? The fabric store, I mean. For quilting fabrics. Hannah's nephew?" Oh, holy mother of fuck, what's wrong with me?

"Yes, Charlie, I know who you are," she says dryly. "Is Hannah all right?"

"Yes, ma'am, she's fine. Everything's fine. I just... Uh, I wanted to let you know that Archie is here and he's fine, but he's asleep. But everything is fine. You don't need to worry." Could I possibly have said "fine" any more times? Why have I suddenly lost the ability to talk like a normal person? After all, I'm only telling the grandmother of the man I love that he chose to come to me during his short respite from fighting deadly bushfires, instead of going home to his family.

She draws in a sharp breath. "Archie's there? And he's well?" Her voice becomes muffled. "David! Ella!"

"He's fine, Mrs Tucker." Oh, hell, that word again. "He's exhausted and he's fallen asleep on the couch, but he's healthy. Uh, he said he has a twelve-hour break, but I'm not sure when it started." Fuck, he'll probably need to be up at sparrow's fart to get back.

I hear a man's anxious voice in the background, and then Mrs Tucker says, "It's Charlie Madden, Archie's friend. Archie's at his house."

The next thing I know, I'm talking to Archie's father, a man I've never officially met, believe it or not. "Hello? Charlie? David Tucker here. Archie's with you?"

"Yes, sir." I break out in a sweat. "Uh, he's asleep on the couch. He's exhausted—was barely coherent when I got here. But he's well. I'm—I'm going to make him something to eat and then just let him sleep until he has to go back. I just thought you'd like to know...."

"Yes, thank you for calling. It's good to know he's safe. Could you.... When he wakes up, could you tell him we love him and we're proud of him? His mother and grandmother and me."

Tears prick the backs of my eyes. "Yes, absolutely," I assure him. "Uh, do you want me to tell him to call you? Or

I could wake him—he needs to eat something anyway and move to a bed. The couch is kind of uncomfortable." I'm babbling.

"No, no. Let him sleep as long as possible. If he has time to call in the morning, that would be great, but we understand he's busy. Thank you again for calling, Charlie. It means a lot. Do you need anything? Is there anything I can get for you?"

I'm beginning to feel somewhat... guilty? After all, it's not like I've done anything special. "That's very kind of you, Mr Tucker, but I'm just going to make something simple for Archie to eat and then let him sleep. I'll be sure to pass on your message. I hope you all rest a little better tonight."

He thanks me again, and then Mrs Tucker (Amelia, the grandmother) gets on the line again and thanks me as well. I haven't seen her this week, what with Archie being away and not able to bring her to the shop, and I impulsively offer to bring some fabrics out to her if she wants. She accepts delightedly, calls me an angel, says we need to *renegotiate our deal*, and hangs up, leaving me wondering exactly what she means and how worried I should be.

I check on the soup, get the toast started, and then study Archie, chewing on my lip. My first thought was to make up the daybed in the second bedroom for him to sleep in, but he's awfully tall. He's not going to rest much better there than he would on the couch, which is an instrument of torture to sleep on—trust me, I know.

No, he'll be best off sleeping in my bed.

I blush hotly just thinking it.

I'm not planning to take advantage of him. Banish the thought. I'll take the daybed. He needs a proper night's sleep before he goes back to fighting fires.

The toast pops, and I butter it, serve up the soup, and

put it all on a tray that I carry over to the coffee table. Then I sit beside Archie, lay a hand on his arm, and shake gently.

"Archie? You need to wake up for a few minutes. Archie? Come on, you have to eat something."

He rouses gradually, then just blinks at me for a few seconds. A slow smile spreads across his face. "Hey. Pretty."

I smile back. He's really out of it. "Hi. Can you sit up? I have dinner ready for you."

He wakes up properly then, shadows filling his eyes as he blinks away the last remnants of sleep. Groaning, he hauls himself up from his semi-recline and looks around.

"Sorry for barging in on you," he mutters. "Ah, what time is it?"

I glance at the wall clock. "Nearly nine thirty. And don't be sorry. I'm glad to see you. Do you think you can manage some soup and toast?" I gesture to the tray on the coffee table, and he looks at it.

"That sounds perfect. Thanks."

I leave him to eat in peace, pottering around cleaning up the kitchen while I eat my own toast, then going to change the sheets on the bed. When I get back, he's finished eating and is washing his dishes.

"You don't need to do that," I chide, and he flashes a smile over his shoulder, looking much more himself than before.

"You cooked. The least I can do is clean. Especially since I'm going to be a really awful guest and go right back to sleep. Uh, if it's okay for me to stay?" He seems uncertain, and I hate that. I never want him to be anything but completely confident about his welcome with me.

"Of course it is. I just changed the sheets, so the bed is nice and fresh."

"I can sleep on the couch," he protests, just like I expected him to, and I snort.

"Believe me, you do *not* want to sleep on that couch. You have to be fit and able tomorrow, and you won't be if you sleep there. I'm convinced the designer was a sadist." I don't give him time to argue again, taking his arm and steering him into the tiny hallway. "This is the bathroom, clean towels under the sink, and here's the bedroom. What time do you need to be up tomorrow?"

"Five," he murmurs, and I wince.

"Okay, well, my phone charger is plugged in next to the bed, so go ahead and use it and don't forget to set an alarm. Do you want something to sleep in? A T-shirt or boxers or whatever?" I tingle all over at the thought of him wearing my clothes... and then realize there's no way he could wear my clothes. He's five inches taller and a lot broader.

He smiles at me in a way that sends those tingles racing, then says, "I'll just sleep in my jocks."

I think maybe I have some sort of neurological event thinking about him in his underwear, sleeping in my bed, because next thing I know, he's saying my name with a concerned look on his face.

I stretch my mouth into a semblance of a smile. "Right. Great. So... I'll leave you to it. Oh—I hope you don't mind, but I called your family and let them know you were okay. Your dad says if you have time in the morning, please call them, but they love you and are proud of you." I almost tear up again just saying it. It's worth it, though, because from the look on his face, it means a lot.

"Thanks," he says quietly. "I didn't think to call them before, but I should have. I'm glad you did."

"You're problem," I reply, then close my eyes and slam my hand to my forehead. "I mean, no problem, you're welcome." My face is burning hot. This is ridiculous. Archie and I talk all the time without me making an ass of myself.

It must be the thought of him + underwear + my bed.

I mumble something and make my escape back to the kitchen. He did a great job cleaning up the last of the mess, so I find my Kindle and curl up on the couch to read for a bit. I hear him moving around in the bathroom, then he goes into the bedroom and silence ensues.

Now that he's settled, I sneak out of the house and race next door. My neighbour, a single mum of two, is amused when I ask her for "anything that could make a decent breakfast," but obligingly provides eggs, bacon, potatoes, and tomatoes. I tell her she's amazing, promise a week's worth of free babysitting, and race back home.

The unit is still silent, Archie obviously sound asleep, so I put the groceries away and settle back with my Kindle again, my ears pricking up at every tiny noise in case Archie needs anything.

I finally manage to focus, and my book turns out to be better than I thought. It's nearly midnight before I put it down, and I take a moment to wish that this new year won't continue the same way it's begun. I check the doors and turn off the lights in the kitchen/living room. Trying to be as quiet as possible in the bathroom is a shocking failure, because every tiny noise seems magnified. I think it's like a law or something that when you're trying to be quiet, you end up being louder than usual.

I swear, it's only because I'm afraid I might have woken him that I peek in on Archie. Normally I would never look in on a sleeping guest, because can you say creepy? But I was like a herd of elephants in the bathroom, so I just pop my head around the door to make sure he's sleeping peacefully.

"Charlie?" he mumbles sleepily.

Well. That answers that.

"Sorry I woke you," I whisper. "I'm just heading to bed. Sleep well." I draw back and start to close the door.

"Charlie? Where are you going?"

"Uh…" I stick my head back in. "To bed?"

The sheets rustle, and in the faint light from around the curtains, I can see the shadow of him sitting up.

I swallow. Hard.

"You can't sleep on the couch," he says. "You said it was uncomfortable."

"Oh, no. I'm not going to sleep on that thing. I wouldn't be able to walk tomorrow. There's a daybed in the other bedroom."

There's another rustle, and then the bedside light clicks on. I squint in the sudden brightness. He does the same. And then my gaze drops from his face to his chest.

His beautiful, sculpted, amazing chest.

I've seen his bare chest before. We're friends, remember? We play sports together. (Well, he plays, I watch.) We've been to the beach together. His bare chest is not new to me.

But it still gets me every time.

"Why are you sleeping in the other room?"

I'm still blinking, because of both the light and his sleep-rumpled awesomeness. "Because you're sleeping in here."

He sighs. "Yeah, I get that. What I mean is, why aren't I sleeping in the other room? I never meant to kick you out of your bed."

"Oh, I know," I rush to assure him. "But the daybed's kind of small, and I wanted you to sleep properly. It's fine." Fuck, there's that word again.

His sigh this time is long-suffering. "Charlie, I'm not

going to sleep well knowing I've stolen your bed." He flips back the sheet, and my breath stalls.

Swimming before. Friends. Seen him. Etcetera.

But holy fuck.

Because his underwear isn't boxers. It's boxer briefs. And they cling to... everything.

I've never seen him like *that* before.

This poor little gay boy might just be having another neurological event.

Then he swings his legs over the side of the bed, and I snap back to reality.

"What are you doing?" I rush into the room and stand there, waving my hands. "Get back into bed. You need sleep."

He looks up at me, his grey eyes warm and heavy-lidded, and I take a deep breath.

"I can't sleep in your bed knowing I've turned you out of it." He stands, and I involuntarily take a step back, because that big, tanned body with so little on is over-whelming.

"Well... what did you think was going to happen?" I scramble to gather my thoughts. Was he so tired when he got into the bed that he just didn't think it through?

He shrugs, and oh my god, the muscles moving and the skin and he has nipples.

Nipples!

"I figured you'd just sleep in the bed with me. It's big enough for us both."

I.

What.

Me.

Bed.

How.

Ungggggh.

There are no words. Where are the words? He's looking at me, waiting for me to say something, but *there are no words coming*. Speak, Charlie! Dammit, speak!

I open my mouth… and whine.

Yes.

Whine.

An actual whine.

I sound like a chastised puppy.

My face goes so hot, I'm convinced the blood vessels in my cheeks are going to rupture.

"Charlie?" He looks kind of amused now, which is just embarrassing, but he's also thoroughly awake, which is what yanks me back to some semblance of human behaviour.

"You need rest," I declare. "Get back into bed and go to sleep. Please, Archie."

He crosses his arms over the wiiiiiiide expanse of his chest, and I resolutely keep my eyes on his face. "Only if you sleep in the bed too."

Eep.

Me, sleep in the same bed as Archie?

It can't be done.

It's just… not possible.

I open my mouth to say so, then see the stubborn set of his jaw and slowly close it again. Because I know that jaw. It only looks like that when he's determined to win. And when he sets his jaw like that, he always, *always* wins.

So I sigh. "Okay, fine." I walk around the bed to the other side and climb under the sheet, then look up at him. "What are you standing there for?"

Chuckling, he gets back into bed, then turns off the

lamp. The mattress shifts a few times as he gets comfortable, but within minutes his breathing is deep and even.

This is just like when we go camping. Sure, we're a little closer together than usual, and there aren't sleeping bags and layers of clothing between us or three or four other people just feet away. And we're not lying on the hard ground, but instead a really fantastic mattress that my mother insisted on buying me as a housewarming present. Along with the super-soft thousand-thread-count Egyptian cotton sheets, because my mother, angel that she is, knows what a weakness I have for fine fabrics.

So... privacy, soft mattress, luxury sheets, close proximity, lack of clothing.... Sure. This is just like camping.

I'm not going to sleep a wink.

Happy New Year to me.

three

APRIL 2020

THE BELL above the shop door chimes, and I look up with a smile on my face. It's been a boring day of inventory management, and I'll gladly welcome a gossipy customer.

Except it's not a gossipy customer.

It's Archie.

My smile becomes a little forced. Not because I'm not glad to see him—I am. I'm always glad to see him. But since that night he turned up on my doorstep—or rather, the next morning, when his alarm woke us to find me twined around him, clinging like a limpet—things have been... weird between us. That's normal, right? If you wake up basically rubbing up on a friend, it's bound to cause some strange vibes.

So yes, I'm glad to see him, but I wish I'd had time to prepare.

"Hey. Aren't you supposed to be working?" I tease, and he grins.

"I took the day off, since I had to work on Sunday. Can you break for lunch?"

I think about it. "I can't leave the store," I say regret-

27

fully. "Aunt Hannah's not here today, and the courier is coming with a delivery. If I'm not here, he'll take it back to the depot and we won't get it until next week... and then your grandmother and all the other Saturday ladies will murder me."

He laughs. "I can't even say you're exaggerating. What if I get us something and bring it back here?"

"Perfect. I'd love a burger." I bat my eyelashes at him exaggeratedly, and he rolls his eyes.

"Burgers it is. I'll be back." He leaves, and I sink onto the stool behind the counter. Phew. At least now I have some time to get myself together.

I'm not going to lie; after he spent the night at my place, I had these vague, unspoken hopes that maybe things would change between us... but I didn't think it would be like this, with this unacknowledged awkward edge. I mean, if a guy turns up on your doorstep when he's tired and traumatized instead of going home to his loving family or to one of his lifelong friends nearby, it's safe to assume that means something, right?

And when that same guy insists you sleep in the bed with him, even though there's a perfectly good daybed next door that you fit comfortably on... well, that means something too. Right?

And when you wake up tangled up in each other, both semi-aroused, and snuggle closer for a moment before reality sets in and you *both* reluctantly let go... that definitely means something.

Or am I just deluding myself?

Because Archie got dressed, ate the breakfast I made, gave profuse thanks, and left without saying anything else. And since then, he hasn't mentioned that night at all.

I guess I could take the initiative. I could bring it up. I

could drag this… this tension between us into the open and demand that we talk about it. I could tell him I'm madly in love with him and don't want to pretend anymore.

But what if he doesn't want that? What if I lose him completely? His friendship is so important to me. And more… most of my friends here were his friends first. Life-long friends. If Archie ended our friendship—

No. I must give credit where it's due. Archie would never "end" our friendship. He would never force mutual friends to choose sides. I know this, because two of his exes are still part of his friendship group. He's not as close to them as to the others, but they're all still friendly.

He'd never end our friendship, but we'd never be as close as we are now.

I just don't have the guts to take that chance. I think I'd rather live with unrequited love and Archie constantly in my life than risk losing that.

By the time he gets back, I'm ready. I'm smiling. Things are *fine*. He's brought me a giant bacon double cheese-burger and twice-cooked fat chips, and I swear, I could love him for that alone. He even remembered the chocolate-caramel thickshake.

We go into the back room, where there's a small table in the designated "food and drink zone"—trust me, food and drink can have an awful effect on fabric—and I'm halfway through my greasy, fattening deliciousness, determinedly not thinking about the effect it will have on my skinny jeans, when he says, "We should go on a date."

One of my delicious twice-cooked fat chips lodges in my airway, and I spend the next few minutes coughing and hacking and wheezing, tears streaming down my cheeks as Archie pounds me on the back and implores me to take a sip of his Coke.

When I finally subside in my chair, I'm utterly limp and exhausted. Who knew breathing was so important?

Also... did Archie ask me out?

I look across the table to where he's taking his seat, lips turned down in remorse.

"I'm sorry," he begins. "I shouldn't have surprised you like that. Unless..." His skin turns an ashy colour. "Um, it *was* surprise that made you choke, right?"

"What the hell else would— Oh. No, Archie, I wasn't so horrified by what you said that choking to death seemed like the only way out." There. That's reassuring without being too eager. What I really wanted to say was along the lines of, "My darling, you've made my dreams come truuu-uuuuuee!"

"Oh. Well. That's good." We sit in awkward silence for a moment. I debate whether it's safe to try eating again, pointedly not thinking about what Archie said and whether or not he's going to follow it up. "So what *do* you think of the idea?"

Point to Archie.

"Of us dating?" Yes, I'm stalling for time. I need to find the right words. This will not be another word disaster.

"Yes. What do you think of us dating? Of going on a date... with me." His focus is all on me, his gaze soft, maybe a little nervous? There's a half smile on his beautiful lips, and I want to kiss it.

"Uh... isn't the point of dating to get to know each other?"

The sentence thuds down like a boot on a redback, smashing the almost flirty atmosphere that was building.

I suck. They might have been coherent words, but they were the *wrong ones*.

"I mean," I backtrack quickly, "we already know each

other better than most couples who've been dating for weeks... or even months. For example"—I wave at the remains of my lunch—"I didn't even need to tell you what to order for me, and you got it exactly right. What benefit will we get from dating?"

He blinks slowly. "I have no idea if you're saying you don't want to be with me or that you do, and you want to skip right to being boyfriends."

Boyfriends. A thrill races down my spine.

I swallow hard.

"I—I think boyfriends might be premature." Where the fuck is this coming from? *Shut up, you moron, Archie wants to be your boyfriend!* "Maybe we should skip to the pre-boyfriend stage of dating."

The corners of his mouth twitch up into a grin. "The... pre-boyfriend stage?"

I nod, my face getting hot. I wish whatever devil has control of my mouth would just vanish so I can eagerly accept the whole boyfriend thing. "Yeah. Not official boyfriends, but not just casually dating, either. Kissing and holding hands and... stuff." Oh, holy fuck, my ears feel like they're on fire. I don't want to know how red they are.

His grin turns lascivious. It's a look he's never directed at me before, and my body responds eagerly.

Down, boy. Not now!

Hopefully later.

"Stuff, huh? That sounds like a great idea. I can get onboard with kissing and holding hands and *stuff.*"

Oh, fuck it. "Why don't you come over tonight?" There's so much blood pumping through the blood vessels in my head that fainting is a distinct possibility. My heartbeat is pounding in my ears.

He shakes his head.

My heart plummets.

"I want to take you out for dinner first. Then maybe we'll go back to yours. But I don't want this to turn into friends-with-benefits or anything. Everyone will know we're… pre-boyfriends, because I'm going to take you out and show you off."

I sigh dreamily. "Okay."

How can a besotted gay boy refuse?

I hate myself for being a cliché, but I change my shirt three times while I'm waiting for Archie to pick me up.

I don't change my jeans—they're my super-skinny black strategically ripped jeans that make my arse look amazing and outline everything else to perfection. These were my clubbing jeans when I lived in Melbourne, and they've hardly been worn since I moved here, because… well, there's not much call for club clothes at the kind of restaurants that pop up in a small seaside tourist town. Definitely not at the pub. But for a pre-boyfriend dinner with Archie, I don't care if I'm overdressed. My face is closely shaved, my hair styled, I've added a sparkly eyeshadow to my usual liner, and my nails are freshly painted. I haven't paid this much attention to my appearance since I moved here.

I wonder where we're going? I hope it's for seafood. It's been a while since I've had a good seafood meal, and since we had burgers for lunch, it's not likely to be that.

I'm going on a *date* with Archie.

Yeah, yeah, I know I said we knew each other too well to date, but what the hell else is it, really? Dinner with maybe afters at my place? That's a big fat fucking date!

Do you know what this means? Archie is *interested* in me. Somehow I missed that this afternoon. But he must have *feelings*, because I know him, and he wouldn't risk our friendship for a quick fuck. Plus, he *said* he doesn't want friends with benefits. He wants to show me off.

Oh, holy fucking shitballs, if tonight goes well, I could end up being Archie's boyfriend.

And just like that, the uncertainty and nerves are gone.

Because that would be perfect.

And of course tonight will go well. Archie and I are great friends. What could go wrong? Lack of sexual chemistry? Pffft. Please. I have so much sexual chemistry just thinking of Archie that I could... I could.... That sentence didn't work out how I thought. Just know that sexual chemistry is not going to be a problem.

There's a knock before I can go too far down that rabbit hole and change the fit of my jeans. My heart goes pitter-pat, because on the other side of that door is Archie, who's going to be my boyfriend.

I grab my keys and race over to whip the door open. A smile breaks across my face. He's so handsome, and he's smiling at me with his whole face. I feel like I'm the most desirable, amazing man on the planet, because that's how he's looking at me.

How did everything change so quickly? This morning, I was too afraid to tell him I wanted more than friendship. And now....

"Hi," I breathe.

"Hi. You look good enough to eat."

I blush. Because *you know* exactly where my thoughts just went.

He laughs—presumably at my red face—then leans down and kisses me.

Thoroughly.

So thoroughly that when he pulls back, we're both panting and dazed. His pupils are blown, his lips wet, and all I can do is say, "Hi."

See? I told you the sexual chemistry would be good.

He clears his throat. "We should have done that sooner."

I bob my head in agreement. "Much sooner."

We stand there staring at each other. I'm *this close* to asking him to come in. We can eat later—I have two-minute noodles and tinned tuna. Add in some sundried tomatoes and parmesan cheese, plus ice cream for dessert, and it's a minimum-effort feast. Plus, we could eat *naked*. Who needs to go out?

I open my mouth to suggest it—

"We'd better go. We have a reservation."

—and close it again. This obviously matters to him. So, we'll go out to eat and save the naked time for later.

I obediently lock my front door and follow him to... not his car. He drives a battered old Land Cruiser that's perfect for taking off-road when we go camping (and wasn't that a shock the first time I went camping with him. I expected a proper campsite with an amenities block. What I got was a packet of Wet Ones for cleaning up and a chemical porta-potty for my "personal" needs—and was told how lucky I was, that last time they'd just taken a spade).

"What's this?" I look around as he opens the driver door of the sleek black Mercedes, stupidly expecting to see his car, like he might have accidentally gone to the wrong vehicle.

"I borrowed Mum's car," he explains. "Thought I'd make the night extra-special."

Aww.

I get in the Merc, and I have to admit, it's more comfortable than the Cruiser. Archie pulls into the street, and it's a smooth ride—until we turn onto the main road *and my seat comes to life*.

I shriek.

The car swerves slightly as Archie startles. "What? What is it?"

"The seat is moving! Oh, holy fuck, the car is possessed!" My voice has reached an octave that may only be audible to dogs, and I struggle to get the seat belt undone. Moving or not, I am getting *out* of this car.

Archie laughs. He laughs so hard, he has to pull over and stop the car. Since I figure he wouldn't be laughing if we were in danger of being attacked by a demonic car, I give up on wrestling with the seat belt and just wait for him to be done.

Finally, he wipes tears from his eyes and subsides, a broad grin the only remnant of his laughter. "Sorry," he manages. "Uh... it's not possessed. When the car turns a corner, the seat compensates. It... well, it basically 'hugs' you so you won't move around too much."

Oh.

"That's such a huge relief." I don't know what else to say. It's hard to come back from a high-pitched shriek and a declaration that the car is demonically possessed.

Archie leans over and kisses my cheek. "It startled me the first time, too." Then he pulls back onto the road, and I'm so lost in a haze of how wonderful he is that it takes me a few minutes to realize we're not headed to the esplanade, where most of the town's restaurants are.

In fact, we're going in the opposite direction. There's really only one place out this way where food's available.

"Where are we going?" I ask nervously. It's entirely possible that I am *way* underdressed.

"To the resort. The restaurant has a great view, and I thought it would be nice if tonight was a bit different from our usual." He pauses. "Plus, my parents want to meet you properly. They've been nagging me about it since New Year's. I told them they could join us for dessert—I hope that's okay."

Well, that clears up the nerves... not.

"Can we go back? I need to change. I'm not dressed for the restaurant at the resort." I know this for a fact. I've never eaten there myself, because since I moved to town there hasn't been occasion for me to spend $200 on a meal *not including drinks*, but some of the locals like to go for super special occasions—graduations, engagements, fiftieth anniversaries... that kind of thing—and I've heard all about how fancy it is. Ripped jeans, no matter how sexy, do not fit the dress code.

"You're fine." He smiles over at me. "You look great."

Well, yeah, but... I don't want to embarrass him. And I'm going to meet his parents. This is not what I would have chosen to wear for that. He's not turning around, though, so I resign myself to being mildly embarrassed and decide I'm going to enjoy the evening anyway, because it's a pre-boyfriend date with Archie.

It's going to be magical. I just know it.

And it is. The resort is absolutely incredible, and I say that only having seen a tiny portion of it. I still can't get my head around spending an undisclosed amount of money for a hotel room, but if I was ever going to do it, it would be for somewhere like this.

At the restaurant, we're welcomed deferentially (with not even a second glance at my outfit) and ushered to what has to be the best table in the place, with spectacular views over the town and ocean. The chairs are plush, with arms that perfectly cup the elbows—I could seriously spend a whole day in this chair. We order the tasting menu, which is prepared with locally sourced seasonal ingredients, and I really can't fault it. There are a few things I probably wouldn't eat again, but that's down to my preferences rather than quality.

And the conversation....

Archie and I have been friends for years. Conversation between us has always been easy and comfortable, even when I'm being an awkward dork. It's still exactly like that, but *more*. Now we have sexual tension and innuendo and playing footsie under the table. We have hot, lingering looks and the memory of how great our kiss was.

This is easily the best night of my life.

I'm feeling mellow and content when the last of our meal is cleared away and our server asks if we'd like dessert.

"Yes," Archie says, "but could you call up to my parents first? They wanted to join us."

She murmurs an assent and moves away, and nerves strike me again. My teeth worry my bottom lip.

"Are you sure this is a good idea?"

He reaches across the table and takes my hand. The nerves instantly settle. "They already love you, Charlie. You called to let them know I was safe and fed me soup and let me sleep in your bed. My mum pretty much wants to adopt you."

I wince. He thinks he's helping, but.... "They haven't actually met me yet. They may change their minds," I say drily.

"Grandma loves you," he points out.

I blink. "She does?" The astonishment in my voice surprises even me. I know Mrs Tucker is kind of fond of me, but that's about it. She still sometimes looks at me like I'm a bug under a microscope.

He chuckles. "She adores you. She talks about you almost as much as I do."

Warmth settles over me. Archie's holding my hand, he's coming home with me later, and Mrs Tucker loves me. Today has been freaking awesome.

I grin. "In that case, what's good for dessert?"

"Well, there's this chocolate fondant..." Archie shoots me a wicked glance. "I guarantee you'll love it. It's gooey and rich and delicious, and it's designed for sharing."

A shiver runs down my spine at the thought of me, Archie, gooey chocolate cake, and no clothes. If only his parents weren't joining us, we could get dessert to go.

And speaking of his parents... they must have been hovering right outside, because here they are, crossing the restaurant toward us with big smiles.

Archie and I stand to meet them, and I instantly wish I'd stayed sitting so they couldn't see my jeans.

"Charlie!" Archie's mum swoops, grabbing my hands and leaning in to kiss my cheek. "I'm so happy to meet you at last! We've been hearing about you for years, but we've never quite connected, have we?"

I'm a little stunned but manage a smile. "It's lovely to meet you too, Mrs Tucker. I've seen you from afar so often and keep meaning to introduce myself, but it's usually at an event, and...." I shrug. Mrs Tucker is often involved in organizing community events, which means she's always running around trying to keep things on track.

"Well, we've finally managed it." She beams at me, then releases my hands and steps back. Mr Tucker moves forward, hand outstretched for me to shake.

"It's so good to meet you finally, Charlie," he says warmly. I've never been this close to him before, so I never realized how like him Archie is. It's uncanny—if not for the age difference, they could be twins. "Archie and my mother speak so fondly of you. She was going to join us but decided she couldn't tear herself away from *Love Island*."

My eyes go wide, and they all burst out laughing.

"I don't like to think about it, either," Archie commiserates. "Let's sit."

So... my worries about meeting Archie's parents are completely unfounded. I really shouldn't be surprised by how warm and down to earth they are—after all, they raised Archie. By the time we're ready to go, Mrs Tucker—or Ella, as she insists I call her—has enlisted me to help her with her bushfire support drive. There's a lot of work going on at the moment to get people who lost their homes and livelihoods settled again, and a lot of man-hours are needed just for the organizational aspect of it. Putting the fires out was just the beginning.

I'm still smiling as I slide into the car. Archie gets us on the road, then looks over at me. "Is it still okay for me to stay for a bit?"

"Definitely," I declare, reaching over to take his hand.

Talk about a perfect evening.

KISSING ARCHIE IS ADDICTIVE.

We're just inside my front door, in the dark because neither of us waited long enough to turn on a light. I don't know how long we've been there, but my shirt is undone and I've got my hand in Archie's pants. My lips feel all tingly, and I'm hot all over.

It's time to take this to the next level.

"Bedroom," I gasp, pulling my mouth away from his. He whines in protest, his lips seeking contact again, but I take his hand and walk backwards, tugging him toward my excellent mattress and sheets. I'm going to have him naked on those sheets and rub all over him.

I don't bother with the light in the bedroom, either. Our eyes have adjusted now, and there's enough ambient light to prevent us from walking into anything. I push him onto the bed, and he pulls me after him, so we end up in a tangled pile of limbs, breathless and laughing and then breathlessly kissing.

"You're wearing too many clothes," he says, breaking

the kiss and trying to pull my shirt off my arms without unbuttoning the cuffs.

"So are you. We need to get naked." We just lie there, wrapped around each other. I don't want to let him go for that long, and seemingly he feels the same.

But his hard dick against my side is driving me mad with want, and in the end, I'm willing to let him go for a few short seconds if it means I can get better acquainted with *all* of him.

"Count of three, we get up and strip as fast as we can," I propose.

He mutters, then says, "Okay. And lube. Is there lube?"

"In the bedside table. Ready? One. Two. Three!" I try to spring up off the bed, but we're still kind of tangled together, so instead I go sprawling over the side and land facedown on the floor.

"Are you okay?"

I hear him scrambling toward me. "I'm fine! Strip! I need you naked." Hauling myself up, I follow my own directive, although getting out of my jeans is an undertaking that can't be hurried. Those babies are tight and get even tighter when I've been *worked up*.

I'm bent over, working the denim down my legs, when I hear his guttural moan. Twisting, I peer behind myself and see him stretched out on the bed, shadows kissing his gloriously naked body, hand working his dick and eyes on me.

Or to be more precise, on the arse I'm presenting to him.

So I give it a little shimmy.

His groan this time ends on a gasp.

"Hey, wait for me!" I yank at my jeans, finally getting them off, then join him on the bed. "This is mine." I push his hand away from his cock, wrapping mine around it instead. He gasps again. "Mmm. Much better." In the gloom, I lean down and lick the head.

Suddenly, his hand is in my hair, pulling me back up to meet his mouth, and with his other arm, he hauls my body flush against him. I wriggle deliciously against all that taut, velvety skin and firm muscle, and he lets go of my hair and reaches between us to unclasp my hand from him.

Before I can pull away from his mouth to protest, he's got both our dicks in his hot, callused hand.

"Better?" he whispers, and I make a choked sound. "Good. I'm going to jack us both together like this, like we're going to be together always from now on, and then after we come, I'm going to kiss you and lick you all over like I've been wanting to for years. And then we move on to round two."

"That's the best plan ever," I mumble, most of my attention on the way his cock is rubbing up against mine, hot and hard and slick with the lube he must have found, his hand wrapped around us both with just enough pressure, working up and down, over and over...

I come so hard that lights flash behind my closed eyelids, my body arching, yelling Archie's name the way I have so many times in my fantasies. I collapse against him, spent, and a moment later, he goes rigid.

"Charliiiiieeee," he hisses, and I kiss the nipple beside my mouth as his hot cum splashes between us.

This is perfect.

And in just a minute, when he can breathe again, he's going to lick me all over like....

Wait.

"Did you say you've wanted me for years?" I ask incredulously, propping myself up on an elbow.

He yanks me back down and kisses me hard. "Yes. Since the day I met you."

I laugh. "We're so fucking stupid. I've wanted you since then, too. Why didn't you say anything?"

He shrugs, and I feel the movement of every muscle. It's *wonderful*. "At first because Grandma told me she'd never forgive me if I made her visits to the shop awkward. She knew right away that I wanted to do dirty things to you, but she made me promise I wouldn't unless I knew it meant more. Then... we were friends. I didn't want to lose that. Then, at New Year's, I realized there was nobody else I'd rather be with, ever, and that by not taking a shot I was just wasting time we could be together. I had to work up to it, but I'm glad I took the risk."

"Yeah. Me too." I kiss his nipple again. "I'm glad we're friends. This means so much more than anything I've ever...."

"I know." His hand strokes lazily down my back. "So, does that mean we're more than just pre-boyfriends?"

Grinning, I say, "Yes. We're more than pre-boyfriends. We're together forever."

And we are.

one golden night

one golden night

Never Have I Ever...

Fin

If I'd known my random comment on the Heart2Heart message board was going to result in a Friday night spent watching an eighties TV show about four old women in their nighties, I definitely would have passed. But here I am, sitting beside a total hottie with a great smile. Maybe this won't be so bad, after all...

Clay

Introducing a newbie to one of my all-time favourite TV shows was always going to be a good time, but when I lay eyes on Fin, it jumps to the top of the fun scale. The viewing marathon becomes breakfast and more, but can I keep his interest once the weekend's over?

Lucky I have a matchmaking biker on my side...

This novella was previously available in the Heart2Heart Volume 5 anthology and only the title has changed.

prologue

H2H MESSAGE BOARDS (AUSTRALIA)

TOPIC: Never have I ever... binge watched *The Golden Girls*.

AJ37: Not more than a few eps at a time.

TimsBits: Only once... when I broke my leg. I started dreaming I was Dorothy.

BlanchesGayBrother: <--- Bitches, please. I was literally **named after a character. I binge it ALL THE TIME!**

TheMuffinMan: I've never even seen an episode.

AJ37: What????

TimsBits: You're kidding! Never? Are you still a kid?

BlanchesGayBrother: This is a travesty! As Blanche said, "I feel like I'm in the middle of some awful dream, yet I know it can't be a dream 'cause there are no boy dancers."

TheMuffinMan: LOL okay. Is it really that big a deal?

AJ37: I mean... kind of?

BlanchesGayBrother: Yes! You need to watch at least one episode. It's a rite of passage. We need a public viewing!

ReadBooks: After much begging from @BlanchesGay-

Brother, we'll be hosting a marathon screening of The Golden Girls season one. Friday night at Read Books & Coffee in Brunswick (Melbourne). Free admission, but bookings essential.

FIN

WALKING from the tram stop to the bookstore-slash-coffee shop, I nearly change my mind for the fourth time about going to this... thing. Movie night? Can you call it a movie night if it's a TV show? Whatever. Do I really want to spend my Friday night watching a sitcom from the 1980s about four old ladies?

I check my watch. It's early still—the screening begins at seven, to allow time for people to eat and get here after work. I could go home, hang out with my roommates, then hit the clubs. Or see what some of my friends are doing.

Sighing, I keep walking. The people on Heart2Heart's "Never Have I Ever" thread were so genuinely shocked that I've never seen a single episode of *The Golden Girls* that it inspired the owner of Read Books & Coffee to host this event. Nobody will ever know if I don't turn up, since I don't use my real name online, but it feels like the least I can do is put in an appearance. Plus, it turns out that those cute quotes my favorite agony aunt—or rather, uncle— uses in the Dear Uncle column for *Queer Pride*, the local weekly LGBTQ+ newspaper, are from this show. I felt kind of dumb when one of my colleagues had to point out to me that the Blanche who's always being quoted is actually a character from a TV show and not a historical figure. My bad.

So I guess it can't hurt to go and watch a few episodes before I bail.

They'll let me bail, right? Or is this going to be one of those intense-fan things where you're akin to a serial killer if you don't watch every episode, wear the T-shirt, and discuss the characters' influences as though they're real people? Because I'm not sure how involved I can get in a conversation about Betty White, even if she is kind of awesome. I mean, sure, I can appreciate that she's an icon, even if I've never watched an episode of *The Golden Girls*. Betty's been in a lot of other stuff. But talking about Betty as her character—whoever that is—is not going to happen. I have a sneaking suspicion some of the people who'll be here tonight are die-hard fans, like that one guy who said he was named after one of the characters. So I'll sit at the back, watch a couple of episodes, then slip out quietly while the night's still young.

"You right, mate?"

I blink at the guy standing in front of me. He's huge and has a distinctly killer-bikie vibe, complete with full beard, head-to-toe leathers, and tattoos on his neck and hands, disrupted only by his wedding ring. I'd be tempted to take a step back and look around for witnesses, but people don't usually ask if you're okay before they beat you to a pulp, so I figure I'm safe.

"I'm good, thanks."

He stares at me. "You sure? You've been standing here staring at nothing for a few minutes now."

"Yeah, uh... I was thinking about going home instead of

to this thing. I don't really need to go, and I don't think I want to, but I said I would and I'm here, so..." Why am I telling this scary-looking dude my life story?

He nods sagely. "Expectations are a bitch, especially the ones we put on ourselves."

I... okay.

"What kind of thing is it? Work? Family? Initiation into a cult?"

A laugh bursts from me, but his solemn expression doesn't change—in fact, if anything, he scowls—so I choke it down. It would be just my luck for him to take offense and peel me like a grape.

"Uh, none of those. There's this TV show screening I said I'd go to, but—"

"Oh, you're going to the *Golden Girls* marathon at Read? Me too!"

I shut my mouth.

"I'm a *huge* Bea Arthur fan. Dorothy is life, man. Who's your favorite?"

Oh my god, my worst nightmare is coming true. I didn't even have to walk in—the fandom accosted me on the street!

"Uh... well, actually—"

"You look like you'd be a Rose boy," he says, scanning me from head to toe, and I'm suddenly supremely self-conscious about my work clothes, even though I know I look amazing. I'm an interior designer, for fuck's sake—I can put together a stunning outfit with my eyes closed.

Well, not really, but you get me.

"I've actually never seen an episode," I confess. "What's a rose boy?" Do the women have a gardener or something? Or maybe the show is a bit more exotic than I thought and there's some kind of ritual sacrifice of attractive young men that involves roses? I could probably get on board with watching shirtless guys get tied up and strewn with rose petals, but it seems kind of a stretch for mainstream TV in the '80s.

My new friend looks confused. "A boy who likes Rose. Wait, you've never seen an episode? Not even one?"

I shake my head, and the next thing I know, he has my arm in a very firm grip and is towing me the last few meters to the bookstore.

"You can't go home," he declares. "No. Nope. I'd lose my gay card if I failed to initiate you into the glory of *The Golden Girls*."

Now I'm back to being worried about the whole cult thing.

There's a discreet chime as he pushes open the door and steers me inside the store. A lanky, bouncy redheaded guy whose face is a constellation of freckles comes over from the counter, clipboard in hand.

"Hi! Are you here for the marathon? Because otherwise, sorry, we're closing a bit early tonight."

"We're here for the marathon," my captor says, and the redhead beams.

"Great! I'm Kevin. What names did you book under?" He brandishes the clipboard.

"Ripper," the giant guy still holding my arm says, and I try not to flinch. His name is *Ripper*? Is that because he rips arms off? Forget leaving early, am I going to be able to leave *at all*? "And this is a virgin," Ripper adds. "I don't know his name."

"Fin Liu," I manage. "Uh, is level of sexual experience important here? Because I'm not a virgin. Like... a lot. A lot not, I mean. Not that I'm a slut—or slut-shaming," I add hastily as they both stare at me. "You do you, right? Not that I'm saying you're a slut... either of you. Just that people should be able to have whatever amount of sex they want as long as it's consensual." Fuck me, what's wrong with my mouth? "Uh, so yeah... not a virgin. Why does that matter, again?"

Kevin is grinning widely, almost giggling, but Ripper just stares bemusedly. "Mate, I just meant you were a *Golden Girls* virgin. Never seen an episode."

"Oh." My cheeks burn. "Ah, yeah. That's true."

He starts to laugh, a deep, booming sound that attracts the attention of everyone in the store. "I guess if you're a *Golden Girls* virgin, I'm a *Golden Girls* slut."

Oh my god. Kevin starts laughing too, and I can't stop myself from joining in. Sure, the joke's on me, but at least my arm's not getting ripped off.

"Are you the guy from the message board?" Kevin asks when he gets himself under control again, checking our names off his list. "There was someone on Heart2Heart who'd never seen an episode, either—that's the reason we decided to have this event."

So much for nobody knowing who I am. "That's me," I admit, holding in a sigh.

"Great! We were hoping you'd come. Hey, Clay!" he yells over his shoulder, then turns back and says, "Clay really wanted to meet you."

He... did? Why? And who even is Clay?

That question is answered ten seconds later when a tall dark-haired guy wearing dress pants and a shirt and looking like every other office worker in the city—in desperate need of a stylist—comes out of the coffee shop half of the store and walks over, eyeing Ripper warily. I instantly go on the defensive—how dare he judge my new friend based on his appearance?

I ignore the little voice telling me I've been doing the same thing. *I'm not a hypocrite, you are.*

"What's up?" Clay asks, and Kevin gestures toward me.

"This is Fin. He's the virgin from Heart2Heart."

Clay's warm brown eyes light up, and he grabs my hand, shaking it vigorously. "Hey! Fin, is it? So glad you came. This is going to be awesome, and you're going to *love* the show."

I ignore the tingles of attraction shooting up my arm, too busy sulking over the way people are so convinced I'll love the show. I mean, there has to be a percentage of people who don't like it—that's just mathematical or statistical or whatever. Common sense. Not all people can like something. So it makes sense that I'm not going to like a show about older women from before I was even born. They have to accept that as a possibility, right?

Unless this really is a cult.

Nah. I'm letting my imagination run away from me.

The door opens behind us, chiming discreetly, and I look over my shoulder to see three people come in, all three wearing *Golden Girls* T-shirts. One of them is also wearing a wig and old-lady glasses on a chain and has an old-lady handbag dangling from their forearm.

Maybe the cult thing is possible.

Kevin goes to greet the newcomers, and Clay squeezes my hand to get my attention back, making me aware he's still holding it. It's nice. "I'm Clayton Devereaux," he introduces himself. He really does have a lovely smile.

"Devereaux like Blanche," Ripper says, and then his eyes widen. "Clayton? No way. Like Blanche's brother?"

Ohhhh, this must be the guy from H2H. He nods, smiling widely.

"My mum is a huge fan of the show. A repeat of that

episode was on TV while she was in labor with me, so..." He shrugs. "I'm named after Blanche's gay brother. Although his surname wasn't actually Devereaux, which is why I'm Clayton Hollingsworth Devereaux."

"That's a great name," I say, unable to resist the urge to low-key flirt with him—though I can commiserate with his name being chosen in an unusual way. My mum was high on painkillers and exhausted after thirty hours of labor when she picked my name, and now I have to live with it.

And no, my full name is not Fin. That's just what I tell people.

"That's so cool," Ripper is saying, and seriously, watching him fanboy over this totally dispels every last shred of fear. He may look fucking terrifying, but clearly he's not. "Ha ha, imagine if your mum had wanted to change your surname to match! I wish my mum had been that creative. My name's boring."

I blink at him. "Ripper isn't exactly an ordinary name," I point out, and Clay coughs.

"Your name's Ripper?"

"It's John," Ripper says. "But when I was a little kid, my dad used to call me 'you little ripper' all the time, and eventually it stuck."

Aw. That's sweet. And so much better than my theory about arms being ripped off.

"I'd a thousand times rather have a boring name like John than mine," I tell him, then wish I'd kept my mouth shut when they both look at me.

"Fin's not bad," Clay says. "It's cute... and suits you."

Oh my... is that interest I'm sensing? Maybe tonight is going to turn out better than I thought. Maybe I can convince Clay to sneak out with me after a few episodes. The beginnings of arousal tingle through me.

"Is that all of it, or is it short for something? Finley? Finneus? Fintan?" Annnnd he killed it.

"Not even close. And that's all I'm saying about it."

He and Ripper look at each other and grin simultaneously. "Finnegan?" Ripper guesses. "I'm not letting this go until I know."

I turn and make it three steps toward the door before Clay grabs my arm. They're both laughing. "Come on, you can't go."

Before I know it, Clay's settled me into a chair in front of the screen. The coffee shop half of the store has been converted into a makeshift cinema. The retractable screen is a permanent installation, so I'm guessing they have screenings at least semi-regularly. In fact, now I think about it, I'm sure I remember seeing notices on H2H and ads in *Queer Pride* for community events here. It's a pretty great space for it.

Clay sits on my left and Ripper on my right. I'm right in the middle of the front row, so even without them flanking me, it wouldn't be easy to sneak out early. I'm sure there'll be a bathroom break at some stage, but honestly... I'm not sure anymore if I want to leave. And it has nothing to do with the show.

"So," Clay says, leaning forward to talk to Ripper and resting his hand on my thigh. The tingle comes back. *Yes.* "Who's your favorite?"

"Dorothy," Ripper announces immediately. "You?"

"Blanche, and not just because of the name. I love that she's shallow and vain but still a good person. It's so different from the way most media depicts vain people."

Oh, now that's interesting. I've seen for myself that there's a fine line between being allowed to pay attention to your appearance and being considered vain. The societal expectation is that you should look good without spending too much time or caring too much about it—especially for men. That's bullshit. If I want to spend hours on my skincare regimen and other grooming, why shouldn't I?

"Right?" Ripper agrees. "I like that she's so open about sleeping with a lot of men. And that the other women accept that about her—sure, they sometimes make some snarky comments, but they still live in her house and consider her their best friend."

"The comments are probably more about the time than their real feelings," Clay adds, and okay, I'm intrigued now. I kind of knew Blanche was a sex-positive person because of the quotes in the Dear Uncle column, but I hadn't put it together with the idea of the character being sexually liberated.

The room fills up while Clay and Ripper chat, and I take the opportunity to sneakily study Clay. Something about him really grabs my attention—probably his complete lack of style. He's tallish—well, taller than me, but that's not exactly a huge feat—with messy dark hair, but not in the deliberate way so many of us strive for, and brown eyes. His features are ordinary, although he has a nice smile, and he looks... rumpled. It's both annoying and endearing.

The designer in me wants to get him out of those awful, off-the-rack, uninspired clothes and into an outfit that would actually do him justice. In a pinch, I could make his current garments work with some alterations and tailoring... and accessories.

On the other hand, he's adorably uncaring about how he looks, and something in me finds that confidence appealing. I take care with my appearance because I like fussing with clothes, not because I give a fuck what other people think—I'll happily leave the house in my pajamas if

I like the way they look—but I know a lot of people judge themselves based on the way others judge their appearance.

Either way, the attraction is there, and if he's up for it, I want to get in his pants. Something good should come of this evening.

He catches me glancing at him and smiles. "I'm glad you came tonight. This is going to be fun." His hand is still on my leg, and he squeezes lightly.

Before I can say anything, Kevin comes to stand in front of the screen and calls for attention. "Hey, everyone! It looks like we're all here, so we're going to get started." The room quiets. "Welcome to tonight's marathon screening of season one of *The Golden Girls*!" He pauses to allow for the cheers and applause. I clap half-heartedly, not wanting to be the only one who isn't. "In case you don't know, the bathroom is through that door"—he points—"and you can use it at any time, though we will stop every three or four episodes for an official bathroom break. The register will be open during those breaks if you want to buy a coffee or cold drink, and we're going to have complimentary snacks at midnight, though you're welcome to eat any food you've brought with you. We just ask that you don't make a mess, and please chuck out your rubbish in the bin provided." He points at that too.

"Great," Ripper murmurs, unzipping his backpack and pulling out a bag of popcorn. He leans toward us. "You can share with me if you want."

"Thanks," I whisper, though I'm still full from the kebab I grabbed for dinner. If I don't leave during the first bathroom break, I'll probably be ready for a snack then.

"If nobody has any questions, we'll get started," Kevin

concludes, looking around. Nobody speaks, so he grins and says, "Hit the lights."

A cheer goes up as the lights dim and the screen comes to life. Everybody seems very enthusiastic, and a thrill of anticipation runs through me.

Honestly, I'm disappointed by the first few minutes. Dorothy seems kind of judgy, and there's nothing funny about it. But then Rose and Blanche come in, and I've got to admit that the dialogue between them all is witty. The set and clothes are dated—waaaaay dated—but those outfits are fabulous just the same. I remind myself that rarely is the first episode of any show the best representation of it— pilots, as a rule, are usually still finding themselves.

Then Sophia turns up and makes me laugh out loud.

Clay nudges me with his elbow, and when I glance over, he's grinning broadly. He leans in and whispers, "Say bye to your virginity."

CLAY

I STAND AND STRETCH, yawning wide. This has been a lot of fun, but it's nearly seven in the morning and I've been folded into that chair for hours with only a few breaks.

Fin chuckles beside me. "Does your jaw actually unhinge when you do that?"

Shaking off the yawn, I smile at him. I'd been hoping the guy from the message board would come, picturing myself in a mentoring kind of role as he was introduced to *The Golden Girls* for the first time, but any sense of altruism went out the window the second I laid eyes on him. He's super cute, with inky-dark hair and eyes and smooth sepia-toned skin. I've got a real thing for stylishly groomed guys, even though I can barely be bothered to make sure my own clothes are clean most days.

"I've always been able to open wide," I say, winking, and he smirks back. "Hey, wanna grab breakfast?" I glance over at Ripper, who's watching us with avid fascination and a wide grin. "You too."

"We'd love to," he declares, and Fin shrugs.

"Uh, sure. My only plans for the day are a nap, so..."

I try not to leer, although if I play my cards right, maybe I can convince him to let me join him in that nap. "Great! I promised I'd help clean up, so if you can just wait ten minutes? There's a place a couple blocks over that does great breakfast."

"We can help," Fin offers, and Ripper groans.

"I'm kind of tired."

Fin shoots him a look that should have him quaking in his books. "This is how our friendship is going to work. You accept invitations to breakfast for both of us, and I volunteer us both to help out. We each honor the other's promises. Got it?"

I bite my lip to keep from laughing as Ripper sighs and hangs his head. He's three times the size of Fin, who looks like a kitten facing down a marauding bull.

"Why are the little ones always bossy?" Ripper mutters, and I swear, Fin actually swells with fury.

"I am *not*—"

"If you both really don't mind helping, that would be great!" I interrupt, mostly because as fun as it might be to watch Fin decimate Ripper, Kevin wouldn't be happy if the store was the site of a murder. Fin subsides with a sniff, and I call Kevin over and tell him to put us to work.

It doesn't take long to rearrange the furniture and clean up the small mess behind the café counter, and soon we're standing outside while Kevin locks up.

"Is the store not opening today?" Ripper asks. "You're not coming back after being here all night, are you?"

Kevin shakes his head. "Nah. Kate's the manager on shift today, but she won't be in for a bit." He checks the door is locked, then smiles tiredly at us all. "Have a good one, guys."

"You sure you don't want to join us?" I offer, but he waves me off.

"It's been a long week. I'm ready for bed."

We part ways, with him strolling toward the tram stop and me leading the others in the direction of breakfast. My stomach growls, and I dart an embarrassed glance toward Fin. There's nothing sexy about a grumbly tummy, and I want him thinking sexy thoughts about me.

He doesn't seem to have heard it, which is good, although Ripper smirks at me, so he probably did. That's okay. Ripper seems like good people. And from the way he maneuvered Fin into accepting my breakfast invite, I think he might be on my side in engineering a hookup between us.

Soon we're settled at a table in the only half-full café— seven thirty is earlier than most of the Saturday morning crowd like to be out—perusing the menu. Well, they are—I know exactly what I want.

"Morning, Clay," Binita, the server, says as she puts water and three glasses on the table. "You're out early."

"Not been to bed yet," I tell her. "Love that color on your eyes." Binita is studying cosmetology with aspirations of being a makeup artist, and she's not afraid to try bold new looks.

"Thanks. It's not too shimmery? The pink came out different to what I thought."

"All I know is I like it," I say, studying her eyes. Is the pink more shimmery than the other colors?

"I love it," Fin exclaims, leaning toward her. "The pink is perfect. I love how it sets off the orange."

She eyes him, taking in his obvious fashion sense and impeccable grooming—seriously, how does he still look so good after staying up all night?—and smiles. "Thank you!

That's what I was going for." She glances over her shoulder as the bell over the door jangles, then turns back and asks, "Are you ready to order?"

Ripper and Fin place their orders, and she heads over to the counter.

"Aren't you eating?" Fin asks me, surprised.

"Oh, she knows what I want." I'm a creature of habit.

"Come here often, do you?"

"Kind of?" Nearly every morning. "I live around the corner. This is my coffee stop on the way to work."

"Great coffee stop," he comments, glancing around. "Where do you work?"

As always when I'm asked this question, I'm faced with the split-second dilemma over how honest to be. This time, I decide to go with part of the truth. "I work for *Queer Pride*."

"Really? As a journo, or back office, or something else?" He seems interested, and Ripper's perked up too, but I'm still not ready to bare all.

"In Features," I say vaguely, then before he can push, I ask, "What about you both? What do you do?"

"I'm an interior designer," Fin says readily. We both look at Ripper.

"I own and run a childcare center."

I have to admit to being surprised. He seems to be a great bloke, but I would have thought protective parents would probably hesitate before leaving their kids in the care of a man called Ripper who looks like he chews nails in his spare time.

He laughs. "You should see your faces. It took a while to build my rep, but it's going good now. I have a lot of multi-kid families."

"That's great," Fin says. "I don't envy you all the licensing hassles, though, dealing with kids."

They divert into a discussion on the specific licenses and registrations Ripper needs, stopping only when Binita brings our coffee.

"So," Ripper says, leaning back after his first sip. "What'd you think of *The Golden Girls*?"

Oooh. I turn my attention to Fin. I'm pretty sure he liked it—I heard him laughing often enough—but did he *love* it?

"It's good," he admits. "I'm not sure I'm at fandom stage, but I'll probably watch more."

"We've sucked you in," I crow. "Just wait, soon you'll be buying T-shirts."

He rolls his eyes, but he's laughing.

"And who was your favorite?" I add.

"Yeah—are you a Rose boy like I thought?" Ripper props his elbows on the table and leans in.

Fin shakes his head. "Sorry, Ripper, you were wrong. It's Sophia all the way. I want to be her when I get old."

"A bitch on wheels?" I tease. I don't know him well, but I can see him having Sophia-like attitude as an old man.

He grins. "People will cringe in anticipated fear when I open my mouth to speak. It'll be epic."

Binita drops off our food, and the conversation shifts. Mostly it's between me and Fin, and a few times I feel bad for leaving Ripper out, but every time I glance over at him, he's just smirking and watching us. I figure he'll butt in if he wants to.

Fin asks me how I like living here in Brunswick, which somehow becomes a conversation about the different suburbs we've both lived in and from there a discussion about the housing market in Melbourne generally (hint:

expensive). That tangents into shops we both like, and we spend a while recommending hole-in-the-wall eateries and bakery-slash-cafés to each other. He's in the middle of enthusiastically expounding on the glories of a Malaysian place near him that does "the best mango pudding, bar none," when Binita comes back.

"Guys, I love you—well, I love Clay. I don't know you, but you said nice things about my makeup, so I'm sure I'd get to love you," she adds, looking at Fin, who smiles.

"I could get to love you too," he agrees. "If only because you do awesome makeup."

"Thanks. But anyway, if you're not going to order anything else, I have to turn this table over. We've got people lined up outside."

I whip my head toward the door, and fuck, she's right. It's no longer too early for the Saturday morning crowds. Then, as I turn back to her, I realize something else: Ripper's gone.

"Is Ripper in the men's?" I ask. I'd have thought I'd have noticed him getting up.

"The big guy?" she asks, and when I nod, continues, "He left about forty minutes ago."

"What?" Fin demands. "He *left*?"

"Why didn't he say anything?" I wonder. "How did I miss that?"

Binita smirks and slides her gaze sideways to Fin, but thankfully doesn't say anything suggestive. "He left this for you both and said to text him so you could get together." She pulls a small piece of paper from her apron pocket and hands it to Fin, who shows me. It's a phone number.

"Okay, well..." Fin seems at a loss. "We'll, uh, let you have the table. Do we pay at the counter?"

I open my mouth to tell Binita to put it on my tab, but she's saying, "Your friend Ripper already paid."

I snap my mouth closed, then pull out my phone and snap a picture of the scrap of paper. I need to text Ripper later and make a time to buy him a beer. The guy let me have Fin all to myself *and* bought us breakfast.

Fin and I thank Binita, apologize for hogging the table, and soon find ourselves out on the street. We edge away from the people waiting and just hover, unsure what to do next. I really want to invite him to come home with me—or failing that, arrange to meet up later. It just feels weird asking in broad daylight in the middle of a busy street. Hooking up is so much easier in a dimly lit bar or club with bass pounding and crowds pressing in on all sides.

He shifts his weight, probably in preparation to walk away, and that spurs me to action.

"Wanna come back to mine?" I meet his gaze directly so there can be no misunderstanding. I'm not offering him another coffee or a debate about which bar has the best-priced drinks.

His lips twitch into a one-sided smile. "Yeah."

I shove open the door to my tiny apartment, yank Fin inside, and slam the door behind us.

"Ooh, I like a forceful man," he mutters as I push him back against the door and plaster my mouth to his. He's a fucking awesome kisser, and for a moment, I'm tempted to just keep kissing him for a while.

Then he slides his hand down my torso and into my pants, and I wave that idea goodbye.

"Strip," I gasp, pulling back. "Bedroom." I take two

steps away, unbuttoning the top few buttons of my shirt, before stopping to wrench it off over my head.

"Move faster," Fin says behind me, squeezing my ass, and I stumble forward.

We leave a trail of clothing from the door to my bed, but I'm not looking at that. I can't take my eyes off Fin. He's lithe and toned and smooth and just as perfectly groomed without his clothes as with them... only now I have the bonus of seeing his cock pointing at me. My own, already hard and aching, responds, getting stiffer and pulsing its need.

I tackle him to the bed. A laugh bursts from him, then he wraps his legs around my waist and bucks his hips, digging his heels into my ass. We both moan deeply as our dicks rub together.

"Fuck foreplay," he gasps. "You got lube?"

I'm too busy wallowing in sensation to absorb that immediately. It's only when he pushes me slightly away that it sinks in.

"Lube! Drawer." I lever myself up, hating the separation from his warm body, and yank open the top drawer in the bedside table. There's the lube, and I grab a condom as well. I'm on PrEP, but I still never go bare with anyone I've just met. PrEP doesn't do anything to prevent chlamydia or a myriad of other STIs, and not to overshare, but been there, done that, don't want the T-shirt—or a repeat.

Fin must be on the same page, because when he sees the condom, he says, "Oh, good," and grabs it, sitting up halfway and nudging me back. Does that mean he wants to top? I'm fine with that, but I was kind of hoping to get into him first. Those well-tailored pants showed off the most incredible bubble butt, and it's been an effort to keep my hands off.

He rips open the condom, then begins rolling it on me. His hand smoothing down my dick tears a sound from my throat, and he glances up at me with a wicked little smirk.

"Just so you know, if we do this again, you might not get to top next time. But right now I want you to master me."

I'm not even sure I know what that means. All I really heard was "do this again." "Yes," I agree, and when he flops back on the bed, lubing up his fingers and beginning to prep himself, I realize it's my turn to act.

Master me, he said. Okay. I can do that. First step: wipe the smirk off his face.

I bend and take his cock into my mouth. From the sound of surprise he makes, he wasn't expecting that, and satisfaction thrums through me. Then I get to work, taking his balls in hand. The skin of his sac is tight, and as I hollow my cheeks around his dick, it gets even tighter. I've been told I'm gifted at giving head, and the noises coming from Fin are very appreciative... and becoming increasingly desperate.

Finally, he smacks my shoulder. "Stop. Gonna c-come."

I pull off. "Come, then."

He shakes his head frantically. "I want you to fuck me. If I come first, I'll be too sensitive."

Oh. Well, in that case...

I let go of his sac, bend forward to kiss him, then grab the lube bottle.

"I don't need more prep," he says, and I cast him a doubtful look. He didn't get the chance to do much before. "Promise," he assures me. "I have great muscle control."

My still-hard cock suddenly becomes a throbbing steel pole. I dump some lube on it, hook my elbows under his knees, and position my dick at his pucker.

"You're going to feel this," I warn, and the slightly punch-drunk look on his face is my reward.

"I want to feel it for days," he promises. "Do it."

I push forward, slowly at first, then more firmly when I feel his muscles adjusting around me.

"Hurry up, fuck you," he gasps, and my control snaps.

I thrust home.

We both moan.

For a second, I just savor the sensation.

Then I ease back, keeping a watchful eye on his face. There's nothing but bliss there as his chest heaves with his gasps. So I adjust his legs over my arms, deepening the angle even more, and go to town on his ass.

After three thrusts, he grabs his cock and begins jacking himself. I watch avidly: right now, he's the hottest fucking thing I've ever seen, with his dick in his hand, his face screwed up in ecstasy, my cock pumping into his ass.

A moment later, he comes, spraying cum over his chest, and that's all it takes to send me over the edge.

FIN

I DON'T LEAVE Clay's place until nine on Sunday night. What started out as a quick fuck turned into a fuck and a super-long nap, since neither of us had slept in nearly thirty hours at that point and we're no longer teenagers. When we woke early Saturday evening, I made noises about leaving, but instead ended up staying for takeout and more sex. I mean, come on—I wasn't going to turn that down. Then we somehow ended up watching a movie, then fucking again... anyway, between fucking, food, TV, and conversation, I don't get around to leaving until I remember I need to iron a shirt for work tomorrow.

Clay offered to drive me home, but it's really not that far, and anyway, wouldn't that be weird? Having my weekend hookup drive me home like he's my boyfriend or something? So I told him I was going to stop by a friend's on the way and left before he could offer to drive me there. He's a real sweetie. We did exchange numbers—even if we don't hook up again, I like him, and new friends are always good, right?

But yes, there is a small part of my brain that's thinking

he could be more than just sex or a friend—or both. I tell that part to shut the fuck up, because I don't have *time* for a relationship right now.

Well... okay, so that's not strictly true. More that I feel like I shouldn't have time? I mean, I'm twenty-eight. My career is going gangbusters. I live in a vibrant city with a decent gay nightlife. Aren't I supposed to be making the most of being young? Focus on work and being sexually unrestricted and having brunch and buying designer clothes, instead of... I don't know. Mortgages and missionary sex with the lights off. How should I know? I've never been in an actual relationship before.

I get on the tram wishing that didn't sound quite so stupid, even in my head. To distract myself, I pull out my phone and the scrap of paper with Ripper's number on it and text him.

FIN

> Hey, this is Fin. Thanks for breakfast yesterday.

He texts back right away.

RIPPER

> Ur welcome. Took you long enough to message... been busy?

He follows that up with an eggplant emoji, just in case I didn't get the innuendo. I can't help but snort.

FIN

> Very busy. Just heading home now.

My phone rings in my hand, and I answer. "Hi."

"For real?" he crows. "You spent the weekend with him? I am the king of matchmakers!"

"It was a hookup," I say dryly. "Don't get carried away, Your Majesty."

"Many a beautiful relationship began with a dirty fuck," he tells me sagely, then, distantly, "No, I'm not talking about ours. I worshipped you from the beginning."

"Talking to your husband?"

"Yep. He couldn't come Friday because of a work thing. And he doesn't like *The Golden Girls*, which is the only thing about him that causes strife in our marriage."

While I'm digesting that, there's a murmur in the background, then Ripper says, "He wants to know if you're going to see Clay again. The answer's yes, right?"

"Probably," I concede. "He's a nice guy."

Ripper whoops. "KING OF MATCHMAKERS!"

I hang up on him. He texts me a minute later.

RIPPER

Dion says you should come for dinner one night this week. He wants to meet you.

Aw. That's nice. I wonder what Ripper's husband is like?

FIN

Wednesday okay?

He texts back a thumbs-up, then an address.

RIPPER

7pm. I'm inviting Clay too.

I confirm, noting he seems to be serious about this matchmaker thing, then shove my phone in my pocket and race to get off the tram as we reach my stop. If nothing else, this weekend has potentially broadened my friendship circle.

When I get home, I can smell the lingering aroma of

something amazing, telling me that one of my roommates —probably Ian, since Lala hates to cook—worked magic in the kitchen for dinner. I wonder if anything's left.

"That you, Fin?" Ian calls.

"No," I yell back because small things amuse me.

"There's leftovers in the oven."

I knew there was a reason I still lived here, despite the tiny room and crappy bathroom. I swear, one day the mold on the walls will come to life. But Ian and Lala are pretty great, the location is fantastic, and having two roommates in a crappy house means more money for clothes.

I head straight for the kitchen. Ian's there, sitting at the tiny table reading a paper. Probably *Queer Pride*, since he has online subscriptions to other papers, but Lala goes out to buy *Queer Pride* every Sunday without fail.

"Had a good weekend?" Ian asks. He doesn't look up from the paper, but there's a leer in his voice.

"Fucking fabulous, with emphasis on the fucking." I open the oven door carefully—it falls off if you go too fast —and gingerly touch a finger to the side of the covered dish. It's warm, but not too hot to touch, so I grab it out and check the temperature of the curry inside. It could probably do with some heating, but it's not cold, and I can't be bothered to wait for the microwave to do its thing, so I grab utensils and join Ian at the table.

"So you didn't go to that marathon thing after all?" He still hasn't looked up, but Ian is the master of multitasking. Don't ever think he's not paying attention.

"No, I did. I met this guy there."

Now he glances up, quirking an eyebrow. "You met a fuckable guy at an all-night viewing of *The Golden Girls*?"

I swallow my mouthful, then point the fork at him. "I object. *I'm* a fuckable guy, and I was there. It was actually pretty fun. People get way too into it, but it was a good night."

He shrugs. "If you say so. I remember watching some repeats with my mum when I was little. It didn't seem that great to me."

"Some of the humor would have gone over your head. There's a lot of innuendo."

Turning the page, he says, "Whatever. Tell me about this guy."

It's my turn to shrug. "Nice guy. No sense of style. Fucks like a champion. I think you'd like him. Oh, hey—and he actually works at that paper you're reading. I think he said Features?"

That gets his attention. "Really? Cool. I wonder if he's written anything that's in this edition. What's his name?"

"Clay. Uh, Clayton Deveraux." I don't usually remember the surnames of my hookups, but he and Ripper both made a big thing about it being the same as Blanche's from the show. I wonder what episode it is that her brother is in— I'm kind of curious to watch it.

Ian flips back and forth a few pages. "I'm not seeing that name, but there are a few articles that just say '*Queer Pride* staff.' And then there's the regular weekly stuff like the Dear Uncle column."

Something niggles in my brain. "Doesn't the Dear Uncle column always quote *The Golden Girls*?"

Ian stares at me, then turns the page so fast, he almost rips it. "There's no name," he reports, scanning the column. I lean across the table, trying to read it upside down. "It's just signed 'Your Gay Uncle.' Hang on, I'll read the first one."

Dear Uncle,

Last year my partner and I ended a fifteen-year relationship, and I'm finally ready to try dating again. The problem is, when I went back to the clubs, I was intimidated by how young everyone seems. I felt old and unattractive. My sister thinks I should get a new wardrobe and a facelift, but that seems drastic. What do I do to avoid becoming a lonely old man?
Thanks,
SaggyBalls

Dear SaggyBalls,
You say you went "back" to the clubs, which leads me to believe you'd outgrown them while in your relationship. That doesn't change now it's over. Look for dates in the places you've been socializing for the past decade—the people there are on the same wavelength as you. You don't need to go clubbing just because you're single.
Blanche once said, "There are lots of ways you can trick a man into thinkin' you're younger than you really are." To that I add: but why would you want to?
Love,
Your Gay Uncle

Ian lifts his gaze to my face. "Well? Does that sound like him?"

I roll my eyes. "How the fuck should I know? Blanche is his favorite, though." I drop my fork into the empty bowl and dig my phone out of my pocket. "I'm just gonna ask."

My annoying roommate snorts.

"What?"

"Nothing. Just... you left his place less than an hour ago, and already you're calling him? I think you're smitten."

I freeze. "First, smitten is a dumb word that only old ladies use."

"You'd know, since you and your new sweetheart spent Friday night watching a *Golden Girls* marathon." He smirks.

"Second," I say louder, ignoring his irritating and absolutely correct jibe, "I wasn't going to call him. I was going to text. And since the text has a clearly defined purpose, it's not weird or eager or anything like that."

"What's not eager?" Lala asks from behind me, and if my dinner dishes weren't right in front of me, I'd be thunking my head on the table.

"Fin's going to text the guy he spent the weekend with," Ian reports.

"*Now?*" Lala demands incredulously. "The weekend's not even over! He's going to think you're a weird stalker."

I sputter for a few seconds, then give up. "I'm going to iron my clothes for tomorrow," I declare, standing with as much dignity as I can muster. "Ian, for being such a turd, you can load the dishwasher."

He flips me the bird as I walk out, and I hear Lala demanding he tell her the whole story. Her name is actually Alexa, by the way. Apparently when she was a toddler, she couldn't say it and called herself Alala, and because her family is a few bricks short of a load, they decided Lala would be her name forevermore. She's cool, though, and anytime anyone at KPMG—where she's a risk analyst—tries to give her flak over her name, she rips them a new one.

In my bedroom, I flop down on the bed and unlock my phone. I don't care what Ian says—texting to ask Clay if he's the writer behind the Dear Uncle column is not the same as just texting randomly because I have a thing for him.

FIN

Hey, just been reading Queer Pride. Are you the "gay uncle" who writes the column?

I put my phone on the bed and go to select an outfit for tomorrow. There's an incoming message alert before I'm done.

CLAY

What gave it away?

I grin, kind of impressed. It's a decent column, and he usually gives good advice.

FIN

Instinct… and Blanche. It makes sense that her gay brother would quote her in every column.

He sends back a string of laughing emojis, and I go to turn on the iron with a smile on my face.

CLAY

I GET off the tram and head down Bourke Street toward the *Queer Pride* office. Monday can be either a great day or an awful one, depending on the response to the latest edition of the paper. My work email and voicemail will be full of messages from people who either loved or hated what I said in the Dear Uncle column—and that's before I even get to the feedback on the stuff I did with the rest of the Features team.

This morning, though, there's a spring in my step. How can there not be, after the weekend I had? I have high hopes for the rest of the week too—I got a call from Ripper last night, after I texted to thank him for breakfast and invite him out for a beer, asking me to have dinner at his place with him and his husband... and Fin. Which means I get to see Fin again Wednesday. And he texted me last night, which is a good sign, right? Even if it was to ask about the column. It shows he's thinking about me.

So yeah, it's kicking off to be a good week.

I stop at one of the laneways and look up. Whatever

business is on the first floor of this building is having a Post-it war with an office in the building on the other side of the lane and winning by a ridiculous margin. They change it up every Monday morning, early—or maybe Sunday night when I'm not around to see. Last week was a flying unicorn shitting a rainbow, which, not gonna lie, made me snort coffee out my nose. Today is much more sedate, a giant yellow duck, rubber-ducky style, swimming along a stream of blue, followed by three much smaller ducks. Aww.

Checking for traffic and trying not to get trampled by the people rushing by, I cross the laneway and turn to look up at their rival's window. It's cute, a winky-face emoji blowing a kiss, but it doesn't have the detail or impact of the first window.

Overcome by an instinct I don't want to examine too closely, I pull out my phone, lift it, snap a picture of the duckies, then send it to Fin.

I lean against the building, staying in the laneway where I'm not likely to get trampled, and watch as *Delivered* changes to *Read*. A second later, Fin texts me back.

FIN

> Are you stalking me? Is this supposed to be a tit-for-tat after I guessed you're Dear Uncle?

I frown at the screen. What?

CLAY

> What? I just thought it's cute and you might like it. Sorry if it seems like stalking.

Pushing off the wall, I try to shove away the sudden gloom. I guess texting him that pic was kind of boyfriend-y

—or at the very least, assumes we're friends, not just a one-time hookup. I can see why he'd think it was weird.

My phone dings again before I can rejoin the morning rush, and I glance at it.

FIN

LOL! So funny, I work for that company. You legit sent me a pic of my workplace with no text, and for a sec I had horror movie flashbacks!

I blink. Seriously? I've been staring up at Fin's office for months now, and it took a *Golden Girls* marathon for us to meet?

CLAY

R u serious? You work there?

FIN

Look up.

I do, and there's Fin, standing at the window with the ducks, peering at me over the babies' heads. He waves, then glances down. A second later, my phone dings again.

FIN

Have a very ducky day!

I laugh, getting a few strange looks from passersby, then blow him a kiss and wave before rejoining the throng and heading in the direction of my office.

Yeah, this is going to be a good week.

FIN:

Are you there?

CLAY:

Depends where you mean by there. Or is this an existential question?

FIN:

Ha ha. You're so funny. Wait… nope.

What ep does your namesake appear in?

CLAY:

My namesake? Huh?

Ohhhhhhh you're watching The Golden Girls!

I KNEW WE'D CONVERTED YOU!!

FIN:

Whatever. It's Monday night, I'm all caught up on Drag Race and The Great British Sewing Bee, and there's nothing else to watch.

CLAY:

You're protesting too much.

FIN:

I'll just ask Google.

CLAY:

No! It's s4e9 and s6e14. Content warning for homophobia but it all comes good.

Are you watching now? Text me what you think at every scene change.

FIN:

Srsly? How about no.

CLAY:

Fiiiiiiiine. You're such a spoilsport.

Soooo… is the first one done yet? It's been half an hour. The ep is only 25 mins.

FIN:

LMAO yes I'm done. Did your mum name you after him because she was crushing on the actor?

CLAY:

…

I've never asked. And thanks for putting that thought in my head.

FIN:

You're welcome!

What are you doing tonight? Aside from obsessing over me watching this show.

CLAY:

Going through some letters for Dear Uncle for Sunday's column.

FIN:

Wow, you bring work home on a Monday night?

CLAY:

Just this and only if the day's been overwhelming.

FIN:

Are they actual letters? Like, on paper? I didn't know we still did that.

CLAY:

Haha no. I just call them that out of habit. Some emails, some DMs through the website.

FIN:

Is it fun? Doing the column, I mean. You get some crazy questions.

CLAY:

Mostly it's fun, and yeah, we get some doozies. We only pick the lighter ones for print, though. Some are really hard to read and need to be referred to a counselor to reply.

FIN:

Hadn't thought of that. Do you have a counselor on staff?

CLAY:

No, but the paper donates to a local LGBTQ+ crisis center, and one of the counselors there handles the really dark messages.

FIN:

Good that those ppl reach out for help. I know it's not the aim of the column, but you're doing good work by giving them a lifeline.

CLAY:

Thanks. I tell myself that whenever the dark ones get me down. Nice to have confirmation :-)

So... you gonna watch another ep?

FIN:

Eye-rolling gif

We have got to find you a hobby.

CLAY:

I have one.

FIN:

Four old ladies who wear their nighties A LOT is not a hobby.

Whoa, if anyone saw that sentence out of context, they'd think BAD things about you.

CLAY:

LOL I didn't mean the show.

There are other sides to me, you know.

I have a varied and fulfilling life.

FIN:

uh huh.

Like?

CLAY:

Well, I spent two days with you not watching the show.

FIN:

Are you saying your hobby is sex? Because I can respect that.

CLAY:

One of them, anyway. Like I said: varied and fulfilling.

FIN:

Wanna come over? It's still early.

CLAY:

Want to be fulfilled, do you?

FIN:

eggplant gif

My roommates are both out.

CLAY:

Address?

CLAY

I GET to Ripper's house bang on time on Wednesday night, six-pack under one arm and a container of gourmet ice cream from the gelateria around the corner from my place in my hand. I'm pretty sure Ripper and his husband drink alcohol, but just in case they don't, I figured ice cream is a safe backup. Ripper had some with his french toast on Saturday morning.

The wait between ringing the bell and the door being opened isn't any shorter than normal, so it's surprising to be yanked inside before I can even say hello.

"Good, you're here, we need to prep."

I shake off sudden ridiculous thoughts of being kidnapped for a sex ring. "Huh?"

"Pay attention, Clay! If we're going to pull this off, you need to be on your game!"

"What game?" I have no idea what he's talking about.

"Ripper, love, maybe let the man get his bearings?" an amused voice says, and I look over to see a well-groomed man who would fit in at any corporate bank—dark suit included—standing in a doorway. "Nice to meet you, Clay.

I'm Dion. Can you defend yourself against Ripper for a few minutes while I change?"

I eye Ripper warily. "Sure." It comes out a lot more hesitant than I planned, but Dion just laughs and wanders off down the hall.

"Come into the kitchen so I can keep an eye on dinner," Ripper orders, and I obediently follow him into what I'd probably consider a really great kitchen if I liked cooking or cared at all about kitchens. He goes to stir something on the stove, and I inhale the heavenly scent.

"This should go in the freezer," I tell him, hefting the ice cream. He abandons the stove to ooh and aah over my gifts and put them away, then mixes me a drink before sitting at the kitchen table across from me.

"Are you ready for this? You need to be committed."

I take a hefty slug of citrus vodka and soda. "I have no idea what you're talking about."

"Fin, mate! I'm talking about Fin and the epic love story the two of you will have. I will be lauded as the emperor of matchmakers."

I laugh. "The emperor of matchmakers? You didn't know either of us before Friday, and our meeting was a coincidence."

"But once we did meet, I saw the potential in you both and sprang into action," he argues, and honestly, it sounds deranged, but he might be right? I mean... he was the one who convinced Fin to stay and then accepted the breakfast invite on his behalf. And then he sneaked away, leaving us to bond.

"Fine," I concede. "You're the emperor of matchmakers."

"Well, not yet. Have you and Fin had any contact since the weekend? What have I got to work with here?"

I'm not usually shy about sex, but for some inexplicable reason, heat rises in my cheeks. "Uh, we've had contact." Thorough, sweaty, repeated... contact. All night Monday, and once in the predawn hour of Tuesday morning. "We've texted."

There's a snort behind me, and I look over my shoulder as Dion comes in. "Nobody sounds that smug about a few texts." He gets himself a drink and joins us, and both of them fix expectant gazes on me.

Am I sweating? I feel like I should be sweating. "Shouldn't Fin be here by now?" I ask, glancing at my watch and wondering if it would be weird to call and demand to know how far away he is.

"No," Ripper says. "I told him to come half an hour later than you so we'd have time for this conversation."

"Has anyone ever suggested you might need counseling?"

"Frequently," Dion tells me. "I love him anyway. So you and Fin have seen each other since the weekend?"

Short of leaving, which I don't want to do because, lack of boundaries aside, I actually like these two, I have no alternative but to answer. "We have. And we've texted. I think you can shelve any plot you have and just let us take things as they come."

Ripper looks unconvinced, but Dion pats his arm and says, "That's great." He steers the conversation to generalities, and I relax.

By the time the doorbell rings fifteen minutes later, I'm helping Dion set the table while Ripper puts the finishing touches on dinner, and we're all laughing over the antics of the kids at Ripper's job. Kids are so funny when they belong to other people and I don't even need to see them.

Ripper goes to answer the door, and I glance sideways at Dion. "Is Fin getting the same welcome I did?"

He chuckles. "Probably not. Rip thinks Fin's more reticent about starting a relationship, so he doesn't want to scare him off."

"I don't know if I'm relieved or offended by that."

"Offended by what?" a familiar voice says, and I mentally tell my dick to behave when it immediately stirs. Turning to face the door, I smile at Fin, who looks delicious still in his work clothes. Although he also looked delicious in trackie dacks and an old T-shirt on Monday night.

"Ripper's insistence on calling capsicums 'peppers.' We're Aussies, for fuck's sake," I improvise, and Fin snorts. I can't believe he bought it, but I rush to change the subject before he thinks about it too much. "Hungry?"

Halfway through dinner, we're talking about Dion's job as a commercial real estate agent when it comes out that his office is across the street from Fin's.

"Have you seen the Post-it battle?" I ask, and Dion's face lights up.

"That's your office?" he asks Fin. "I love it!"

"Love what?" Ripper demands, and I pull out my phone and show him the photo of the ducks. "Fucking awesome," he declares. "Is it like an office thing, with a team working on it, or just one person?"

"A bit of both," Fin admits. "It started because I was really stuck on a design concept one day. I needed a distraction, and the office across the lane had 'Hi' spelled out in Post-its in their window, so I did a waving stick figure in ours—"

"Wait," I interrupt. "You're the one who does it? By yourself?"

"I did the first few," he corrects. "Now I come up with

the concept, but the design layout and actual sticking is done by a team of us. The boss liked the attention it got and figured it's worth the time we spend on it."

"You're so talented," Dion says, and I agree. I've been looking at that window every week for months, and the scope of what each design does with only Post-it Notes is incredible.

Fin smiles. "Thanks. It's a lot of fun, I've gotta say."

"Do you get your creativity from your mum who gave you a name so weird you won't even tell us what it is?" Ripper asks, mock innocently, and Fin laughs.

"Definitely. Fuck knows my dad doesn't have any creativity at all."

There's an expectant silence while Fin ignores all of us watching him.

"Is it Finbar?" Dion's the first to break.

"We're not doing this," Fin rebuts, putting down his fork, but there's a tiny smile on his pretty pink lips.

"Finch? Was she into birds or something?" Ripper suggests.

I rack my brain for a name with "fin" in it. "Fingal?"

Fin just sits there, grinning now, gaze on his plate.

"Finnian?" Dion tries, and Ripper scoffs.

"You're just making up sounds now!"

"It's a real name!"

"Griffin?" I try, ignoring the now bickering married couple. Maybe we've been too focused on "Fin" being the first syllable.

A muscle under Fin's eye twitches. I'm not the only one who sees it, because the argument ends instantly.

"Serafino?" Ripper tries. "Or... Infinity? Is your mum a spiritual type?"

Fin sighs. "Do you all seriously want to know?"

"Yes!" We say it loudly and in unison.

He mumbles something under his breath.

We lean in closer.

"What was that?" Dion asks.

Huffing, he looks up and says, "It's Muffin."

Ripper's jaw drops. I swallow hard, trying not to choke on my own saliva.

"Muffin?" Dion repeats faintly. "Your mum named you Muffin?"

Fin nods glumly. "Now you see why I try not to tell people."

"It could be worse," I try to console him. "She could have named you…" I cast around for something that would be worse than Muffin.

"Gonorrhea," Ripper suggests helpfully, and Dion legit spits his drink across the table.

"I'm so sorry," he gasps as we all jump up. Thankfully, we only got lightly misted rather than drenched. Napkins and tea towels are passed around, and Dion uses one to smack Ripper. "Gonorrhea?" he hisses.

Ripper shrugs, stacking our thankfully empty plates so he can wipe the table.

"Just picture how bad that would have been," I tell Fin. "We'd all be calling you… uh… Rhee?"

He snorts. "Yeah, thanks. Super helpful. Next time I make an insurance claim and they accuse me of fraud because I'm 'clearly using a made-up name,' I'll tell myself 'at least it's not Gonorrhea.'"

A squeaking sound escapes me as I try not to laugh. "That's awful," I manage. He's smiling again, so I know he's not upset.

"I'm used to it. I keep a pic of my birth certificate in my

email drafts folder to deal with the official shit, and not many other people know that it's not just Fin."

Dion waves us back to the now clear (and clean) table. "Do you guys want coffee? Or another drink? Ripper's sister gave us this really posh muscat for Christmas. We could open that."

"And pour it over the ice cream Clay brought," Ripper adds.

"Sold," Fin says immediately. "Make mine a double. I'm not driving."

"Seconded," I agree, since I'm not driving either. "Have you ever thought about changing your name legally? Making it just Fin?"

"All the time," he admits. "I even filled out the forms once. But since Mum picked it when she wasn't thinking straight, Dad and the nurses thought she might change her mind once she'd had some sleep, so they waited to fill out the form."

"She didn't?" Dion asks, putting a tall, slim bottle of alcohol and a stack of bowls on the table. Ripper follows with the ice cream and spoons.

Fin shakes his head. "Nope. She thought about it, but then decided it was the name that came to her when she first saw me, so it must mean something. Part of me wants to respect that. Mostly everyone calls me Fin anyway, so..." He shrugs. "It's only a hassle with official docs."

My heart melts. It's so sweet that he puts up with a name he hates just because he doesn't want to hurt his mother's feelings. Under the cover of the table, I slide my hand into his and squeeze. He looks over and meets my gaze, and a light wash of pink creeps over his cheeks as he squeezes back.

Ripper puts a bowl of ice cream in front of me, and even

though he doesn't say anything, I can tell by the massive grin splitting his beard that he knows we're holding hands. I roll my eyes and let go to dig into dessert.

It's not that late when Fin and I say our goodbyes and leave Ripper and Dion's charming little house. The front door closes behind us, and I turn to Fin. "Tram or Uber?"

"Tram. It's not that far, and it's a nice night." He starts down the extremely short front path to the gate. Ripper and Dion have a tiny yard at the front of their house, although I guess the six-foot privacy fence and gate would make it a courtyard? "Am I coming back to yours?"

Yessssss. "If you want to," I say as casually as I can manage.

He side-eyes me, one hand on the gate latch. "I want to. Or..." He glances around speculatively. "Maybe we could just..."

It takes me a second to realize what he means, and then my eyes go wide. "Here?" I hiss. That should not make me as hard as it does.

His grin is wicked as he lets go of the latch and grabs my hand, directing me to stand against the fence. "Why not?"

"You don't think it would make us bad guests?" *Oh fuck, please convince me to do this. I really want this.*

He undoes my belt, and the rasp of my zipper going down sends a shiver through me. Leaning up on his toes, Fin brushes a light kiss across my lips. "You heard Ripper say they spend most of their time at the back of the house. If they do go into one of the front rooms, you'll see the light go on. And nobody else can see us behind this lovely fence." He slides slowly down to his knees, extracting me from my underwear, and I let my eyes drift closed as his hot breath washes over my sensitive skin.

Then snap them back open. I have to watch in case the lights go on.

Fin looks up at me, and the sight of him on his knees, perfectly tailored and groomed, my cock in his hand, his dark eyes gazing up at me... I swallow hard.

"I'm on PrEP and get tested regularly," he says, and my head spins. We've used condoms religiously so far, so this... this is a sign of trust.

I clear my throat. "Me too. I'm negative."

Fin's lips close around the head of my cock, and I try not to let my eyes roll back. His mouth is hot, wet, and my god, the man knows exactly how much suction is needed. His hand is wrapped around the base, the pressure *perfect*, and when he draws back to lick me like an ice cream, my whole body jerks, my foot bumping against the planter beside me. It moves, making a loud scraping sound, and he lifts his gaze to me.

"I thought you were worried about being caught? Maybe that's what you actually want. Maybe I should be making noise, trying to lure Ripper and Dion out here..." His hand slides over my dick, jerking me, and I whimper, eyes wide.

I do *not* want Ripper and Dion coming out here and catching me with my pants down. But I can't deny that the thought of it makes me so hard, it hurts.

Fin must be able to tell, because he grins at me, then turns his attention back to sucking my brain out through my cock.

My head falls back against the fence, and I squeeze my eyes closed. The fresh, balmy evening air kisses my bare skin, Fin's incredible mouth and hands draw me ever closer to heaven, and I honestly can't remember a single moment in my life that was better than this.

Bang!

I jerk my head up as beside me, the gate rattles. "What—"

Fin winks at me, drawing his hand back to slam against the gate again.

"*What are you doing?*" I hiss, my gaze darting to the house. The front windows are still dark, so hopefully they didn't hear—

Bang!

—but they will if he keeps doing it. My cock jerks in his mouth, and while I frantically look toward the house, he slams his hand against the gate again.

"Is everyone okay in there?" someone calls from the other side of the fence, and Fin's eyes widen.

I come.

There's no way to stop it; I barely have the chance to slap my hand over my mouth and hope that'll muffle the sound of me coming so hard, I think I might actually die.

By the time I can breathe again, it seems the passerby has moved on. Fin is still kneeling in front of me, carefully tucking me back into my underwear. He glances up as I heave a sigh and let my hand drop to my side, and he licks his lips.

"That was a nice nightcap."

A snort bursts out of me. "Do I get one too?" I offer a hand to help him up, and he takes—

"What's going on out here? I thought you guys left ages ago."

Fin's gaze clashes with mine as Ripper's voice cuts through the courtyard.

"*Oh my god,*" he mouths.

"Are you fucking in my courtyard?" Ripper exclaims as a floodlight comes on, illuminating us. "Fuck you, you're defiling my azaleas!"

I'm frozen in panic even as laughter bubbles up inside my chest, but Fin's got his wits still. He yanks me away from the fence, jerks open the gate, and shoves me through. "Bye, Ripper, call you soon! Thanks for dinner!" The gate slams closed before Ripper can reply, but we hear him swearing as we race away, giggling.

"Well, that killed my boner," Fin says dryly when we reach the tram stop.

"You can only blame yourself," I tell him. "What the fuck, mate? I nearly had a heart attack when you hit the fence."

"You nearly came," he corrects. "Although I gotta admit, I didn't think it was loud enough for them to actually hear."

"Do you think he'll forgive us?" We were kind of rude.

Before Fin can answer, both our phones chime. We exchange glances, then dig them out. It's a message from Ripper.

RIPPER:

Next time, we're eating at your place.

"I think he's already forgiven us and is now plotting how to get us back," Fin says dryly.

The tram approaches, rattling along the tracks, and he looks up at me. "Am I still invited back to your place?"

Fuck yeah. "Definitely. Let's see if we can resurrect that boner."

epilogue

FIN

ONE YEAR LATER

"WE'RE ONLY STAYING for a few episodes," I insist as we approach Read, mostly just to get a reaction. I know full well we're staying all night. I'm actually looking forward to it.

"No way," Clay denies immediately, just like I knew he would. "We're in it for the whole thing. How could you want to leave early? This is practically our anniversary."

"Our anniversary was two weeks ago," I remind him. "And we have a lot of shit to get done this weekend. Do you really want to help me move on no sleep?"

Clay sniffs and reaches for the door handle, and I take a second to admire him. Over the past year, I've been sneaking bits and pieces of clothing into his wardrobe. I love to shop, and I just couldn't resist buying stuff that I knew would look great on him. A few months ago, he finally told me I was in charge of dressing him and would I please write him a list so he knew what went together. Since then, he's reported being complimented on his clothes by people passing in the street, his colleagues, his boss, and—most excitingly—by a clothing designer who was at the *Queer Pride* office to discuss advertising. He proudly tells everyone his boyfriend dresses him and then mentions I'm an interior designer and hands out my card.

No joke. My guy is super proud of me, and my boss is thrilled because we've had three new clients come from Clay's referrals.

And now we're moving in together.

Honestly, it probably wouldn't have happened for another year. We'd vaguely talked about it but are both busy with work and not prepared to deal. But then two months ago, Lala announced that she was being seconded to Singapore and we'd need to find a new roommate. Ian and I talked about it a lot and decided that since our lease was up soon after she left and our place was a dump anyway, we'd look for something smaller and not bother trying to find someone new.

Then Ian got hit by a car. He's okay, but he'll be off work awhile and needs someone to help him while he recuperates, so he's moving back to Bendigo to stay with his folks for a bit. It won't surprise me if he stays there permanently —he's always liked it better than Melbourne, and he's not really attached to his job. I'm really going to miss him, though—and Lala.

Faced with the prospect of needing to either find new roommates or a place I could afford on my own, I was thrilled when Clay told me he'd be heartbroken if I didn't move in with him. I've never said "yes" faster to anything in my life. It really is sensible, since I already spend half the week with him anyway.

"Are you coming?" he asks, holding the door open, and I smile at him. He's so precious. As I walk past, I rise on tiptoe and kiss him.

"We can stay all night."

He catches up to me before I've taken three steps, swinging me into his arms and planting a big smooch on me.

"I love you," he murmurs, and as always, the words send a thrill through me.

"Love you too."

"Hey, stop with the PDA," a voice demands, and we both turn to glare at Ripper. He's developed this uncanny ability to turn up whenever we're being romantic in public. I think he does it on purpose—he's never forgiven us for "defiling his azaleas."

Kevin is with him, grinning widely, clipboard in hand. "This is a family environment," he says primly. "No tongue."

Clay flips him the bird, kisses me again, then goes to help set up. We came a bit early for that reason.

Ripper smirks at me. "Happy anniversary."

I roll my eyes. "Our anniversary was two weeks ago. Remember? You sent a singing telegram to both our offices declaring yourself the emperor of matchmakers."

He laughs. "Oh, man, that was the best! It was so worth the bribe to get your boss to record your face."

"I could've lived without it," I say dryly, but I can't hold back my smile. With a buffer of two weeks, it's actually pretty funny.

"Anyway, I meant happy losing your *Golden Girls* virginity anniversary," he says, and I shake my head.

"That was two weeks ago too."

"But the marathon is tonight, so tonight's the anniversary."

I really want to point out that anniversaries don't work that way, but it's not worth arguing with Ripper. The only person who ever wins arguments with him is Dion.

"Let's go help," I say instead. "I'm not sitting at the front this time—I want to snuggle with Clay on the couch at the back."

Ripper points a huge finger at me and scowls terrifyingly. "Do not defile the glory of *The Golden Girls* by making out during the screening."

It's my turn to smirk. "Try and stop me." Although probably Clay won't do it anyway. Even though I've now seen every episode and will admit to liking the show, despite its issues—and it definitely does have issues—he's much more enthusiastic.

We get the furniture rearranged and help Kevin check people off as they arrive. If he charged admission, he'd make a fortune—the event was totally sold out within a day after he announced it. But he insists he wants the store to be a community space and that the money he makes off selling coffee and snacks during the event is enough. Which, considering how much he charges for coffee, is probably true.

Finally, I snuggle with Clay on the couch that's been pushed against the back wall. It's a big one, so Ripper, grumbling about boundaries and public places, is grudgingly sitting on Clay's other side.

Kevin stands at the front of the room and calls for attention. "Hey, everyone. Thanks for coming to the second annual *Golden Girls* season one marathon!"

As the crowd hoots and hollers, I think about how I very

nearly didn't come last year. How the only reason I was even on the H2H app that day was because I was bored. How I nearly didn't bother commenting on the thread.

Thank fuck I did.

Or never would I ever have been this happy.

out of the office

out of the office

Who would have guessed achieving career goals could be boring? Not Duncan Witten. But here he is at forty-one, in his dream job... and hating it. Throw it all away for a challenge? Yes, please!

If only Dunc had known his challenging new job came with Paul Hanks, a man who redefined "stubborn." They need to work together to meet targets, but thanks to Dunc's idiot predecessor, Paul won't take his calls or reply to his emails.

There's only one solution: travel across the country and confront Paul face-to-face. It's time to take things out of the office.

glossary

Telco: Telecommunications company. Applies to retailers like Vodafone etc. as well as the companies that build the actual networks

RM: Resource Manager, responsible for identifying people with the correct skills and assigning them to projects; ALSO Resource Management, the department/function.

Project RM: a resource manager assigned to work on a specific project

PM: Project Manager, coordinates a project or subproject within a program of works

PD: Program Director, coordinates a program of works

RA: Resource Administrator, reports to RM and handles administrative duties

Embargo: an Australian government mandated period during which no works can be undertaken on telecommunications networks

Spit the dummy: have a tantrum/meltdown

Hot desking: working from available desks on a time share or rota basis rather than being assigned a permanent desk.

Popular in companies where employees can work from home or other offices/sites.

one

SEPTEMBER 13

THE PHONE RINGS.

It's nearing the end of an ordinary—perhaps even dull—workday, and this is the first time the phone's rung in hours. I snatch it up with enthusiasm. When I finally achieved my goal-before-forty job as Director of Resource Management for a major telco, I never thought I'd end up bored.

"Duncan Witten," I answer, not even bothering to check the display first.

"Dunc, it's Krista. How are you?"

Ah. I lean back in my chair, a tiny smile playing over my mouth. Not to be a dick, but I'm not surprised by how exhausted Kris sounds. Rumour has it that the major project her company is rolling out has run into some big issues and that they begged her to come back early from maternity leave to get resourcing back on track.

"Pretty good, actually. And you?"

"I'm shit," she says bluntly. "Don't fuck with me, Dunc. I know you'll have heard that things aren't going well here."

"Yeah." I'm genuinely sympathetic, especially since the

problems aren't Krista's fault. She left to have her baby about two weeks before the contracts for this project—dubbed Titan—were signed. As Director of Resource Management for another major telco—the competition, and the one with most market share—she was diligent about finding someone to handle things while she was away. I know, because she discussed the options with me—confidentially, of course. We may work for competitors now, but we've worked together heaps of times in the past, and we're friends.

Unfortunately, her replacement was involved in a serious car accident only two months into the twelve-month contract—just as the resourcing for Titan was ramping up and before she was able to appoint a resource manager for it. The HR department quickly hired someone else, but sadly he and the project RM he brought in were useless. Resourcing got more and more out of control until finally the program director spat the dummy in what I heard was an epic meltdown—the kind of thing you only see on "reality" TV. Both temp RMs were shown the door, and Krista was summoned back immediately to try to sort shit out and find a new project RM.

I guess that's why she's calling now—to ask my opinion on the new candidates. If none of them are any good, I can probably help her find someone who is.

"Whatever you've heard, it's worse," Krista announces, and I can't help it: I snort.

"I don't think so, Kris. What I've heard is pretty bad."

"The project is already overbudget and it's entirely due to resourcing."

"It's not unusual to underestimate resourcing costs for a project this big," I remind her, picking up a pen and flipping it between my fingers. "Once the first stage is rolled out, things will settle and—"

"No, Dunc. We're not overbudget on resourcing. Well, we are, but that's not what I meant. I meant the *project* is overbudget, and it's entirely due to resourcing."

I sit up straight. *No fucking way.* It's a multibillion-dollar project. For it to be overrunning the budget because of *resourcing*? What the fuck have the RMs been doing? And how did the project managers and program director allow it to happen?

"That's not good," I manage. Poor Krista. "Have you got a candidate in mind for the project RM?" If things are that bad, she needs to get someone in the role ASAP.

"Yes, I have the *perfect* candidate in mind. He's got fifteen years' experience in resourcing, over twelve as a resource manager, and more than half of that in telcos. He's handled national rollouts like this before and actually knows most of the PMs and line managers involved."

"You're right, he sounds perfect," I agree, wracking my brain. Who the fuck is she talking about? Most of the people who even come close to fitting that profile are women. The only men are Tyler Harris, who is currently working in the US, and—

I drop the pen. "You'd better not be talking about me!"

"Just listen, Dunc," she pleads. "I'm desperate. Beyond desperate. The RM who was appointed had his head so far up his arse that he was seeing the world from inside his own mouth."

I choke back a laugh, because that shit is funny but I don't think Krista is in the mood for a chuckle.

"And the guy who was supposed to be filling in for me.... It's not just Titan that's in trouble right now. Everyone is pissed off. My team was doing their best, but that moron was pulling people off projects for Titan without getting permission. Team leaders have lost confidence in the department, and it's basically anarchy here. The agencies smelled blood in the water and have moved in for the kill—line managers are hiring from everywhere, paying way above the odds for contractors, and meanwhile, our preferred agencies are screaming because the contracts are going elsewhere. I *have* to focus on cleaning up my department and settling this mess; I don't have time to sort out Titan and do the resourcing there."

Wow. That's even worse than I heard. And the thought of uncontrolled agency use.... I shudder. Recruitment agencies and contract staff are essential for huge projects, but the agency percentage can blow out a project budget real quick. That's why most big companies use preferred agencies with a negotiated special rate and build their project budgets around that rate. No wonder the project is overbudget.

Still, not my problem.

"I agree," I say calmly. "So you need to find a good RM to handle that for you. That doesn't mean me, Kris."

"Please," she begs. "Duncan, I don't know anyone else who could clean this up. Right now, I need someone I can trust completely, and more importantly, someone the PMs and line managers will trust. They know you and they *like* you. Just having you come back will make things better."

"Krista, think about this. You're asking me to take a demotion for a contract role—" I quickly calculate how long the project likely has left. "—for eighteen months. *Plus*, the whole project is a shitstorm, and taking it on would be a major migraine. Why would I want to do that?" Maternity leave and stress must have done something to her brain. Normally she's the sharpest tool in the shed, but she seems not to be firing on all cylinders today. "You should ask someone else. Maybe Angie—she'd be up for it."

"It has to be you," Krista insists. "The contract will be a guaranteed two years, plus an additional year if the client takes up the options in the project contract—which they will if the rollout goes well. As to your current job.... Come on, Dunc. We both know there's nothing interesting going on over there right now. It's all maintenance contracts and minor upgrades. Titan is the most exciting project going, and it's right up your alley. You've always been an in-the-thick-of-it type of guy—without a major project to oversee, you're probably bored out of your mind. You need a challenge."

I wince, glad she can't see me. That comes a little too close to what I was thinking earlier. "I still think you should offer it to Angie," I insist, even as a tiny, seditious part of my mind races, weighing options.

Krista sighs. "I can't," she admits. "Any other time, I would. She'd be brilliant for this job. But you know what the rural site supervisors can be like on a national rollout. I have no doubt Angie could eventually wrestle them into submission, but we don't have *time* for that. I need someone who can ensure their attention and cooperation from the get-go. Well, as much as anyone could," she adds. Rural site supervisors are usually complete wankers to anyone from head office who isn't actively working on site with them. And it's worse—much worse—if that person is female. I hate to give credence to stereotypes, but the guys on the line in some of the more remote areas are the reason for those stereotypes.

Added to that, growing up on a station in the outback means I know what the fuck everyone's talking about regarding problems specific to rural sites and can hold my own in most of those conversations. It's something I've leveraged often. For a lot of the guys in the industry, man + engineer + rural upbringing = okay bloke.

So while I don't like that it's true, I can't actually argue with Krista. It *would* take Angie longer to get what she needed from the site supervisors than it would take me. Chances are that I already know about half the rural site supervisors on Titan.

"Come on." Krista, no doubt sensing that I'm weakening, moves in for the kill. "You know you want to do this. This kind of project is what you love best, and rescuing it from the hell it's in now? If you pull this off, you'll be a legend. You love a challenge."

"If I fail, I'll be the guy who fucked it up," I point out, but she immediately makes a rude noise.

"No, because everyone already knows it's fucked up. The PD has all but given up on meeting the first deployment target. He and the CEO are currently scrambling to explain to the board that we'll be paying the client penalties. His job's on the line right now, and he's basically told me to promise you anything."

"Me, specifically?"

"You specifically," Krista confirms. "He took one look at the list of candidates and picked you. I told him you were in a permanent job, and he said we'd pay out your four weeks' notice as a signing bonus, and that your contract rate would allow for the fact that we can't give you the benefits of a perm job. There's a team of RAs to work under you, and he'll personally advise all the PMs that they're to cooperate. Two-year contract, option to extend for a third, credit account for expenses so you won't need to submit expense reimbursement requests. And a fantastic addition to your CV, plus a challenge you can get your teeth into. And believe me, Dunc, there are some real challenges here." She mutters something else that sounds like... *thanks?*

I hesitate, trying to tamp down the little curl of excitement in my gut. It's bloody tempting. Three years is as long as I've stayed in any job before—too long at any company becomes boring after a while; that's what's so appealing about project resourcing—so the longevity of the role doesn't bother me. It's the kind of project I'd give my eyeteeth to work on. My company bid for the job, and we came so damn close to getting it. Working on the bid got me really excited about the prospect of rolling this project out, and I'll admit, I was disappointed when we missed out. And the contract sounds pretty sweet.

"What rate?"

She tells me, and I have to hold in a whistle.

"Let me think about it tonight," I finally say, even as part of my brain is chanting "yes yes yes yes." I need to be a rational adult and think about the pros and cons. Aren't I supposed to be settled and happy in my permanent senior management job by my age? Not leaping into contract roles at the drop of a hat. "I'll call you first thing in the morning."

"I'm going to have HR draw up the offer. If you say yes, we need you here as soon as it's signed."

two

SEPTEMBER OCTOBER

"HI PAUL, *this is Duncan Witten. I'm the new resource manager for Titan. I just want to touch base and maybe see what we can do to get project expenditure down. Give me a call back."*

"Paul, Duncan Witten. I'd hoped to grab a few minutes of your time after the status meeting this morning, but we must have been disconnected. I need to talk to you about the agency resourcing. Can you call me back?"

Hey Paul, I have a plan for project resourcing that will help the budget. Can you call, text, or email me, please.

To: Paul Hanks <epaulhan@globaltelco.com>
From: Duncan Witten <cdunwit@globaltelco.com>
Subject: Titan Resourcing – resource expenditure reduction

Hi Paul,

Hope all is well with you. I know things are crazy busy right now, but I'm sure you see the importance in reducing expenditure and getting the project budget under control. Can you please call me at your earliest convenience? See attached detailed resourcing plan to look over in the meantime.

Thanks and regards,

Duncan Witten
Resource Manager
Project Titan

three

OCTOBER 29

"SO IN SUMMARY, you guys freaking rock and you should be incredibly proud of yourselves." I look around the meeting room at my team of resource administrators. I've pushed them hard since I took over, and they've stepped up to the challenge. There are eight of them, all young, hard-working, and determined, and they were actually doing a pretty good job despite the idiot they had to report to. With a little direction and someone behind them who has the weight to take on managers (that's me), they're doing brilliantly.

With them handling the regular project resourcing, I've been left mostly free to fix the fuckups that had already happened: namely, the massive expenditure on agency resources. On my first day, I had an hours-long meeting with Jimmy Henderson, the program director, and he took me through every resourcing element of the program and subprojects. He's stressed out of his mind because he already had a monster problem even before the budget issues took over. NSW, Vic/Tas, and Queensland are all about two weeks behind schedule—except they're not. Confused? It's actually pretty simple.

According to the contract with the client, the first stage of the rollout needs to be completed by the end of this year. Unfortunately, the bloke in legal who put together the contract and checked the details is relatively new to working in telcos, and for him, the date specified for stage one and the number of weeks needed didn't match. He thought it was an error and changed the date to match the number of weeks, setting the deadline at December 30 instead of January 21.

Why is this a problem? One word: embargo. People like to get in touch with loved ones a lot over the holidays. Networks aren't built to handle that level of traffic—ever sent a text message at midnight on New Year's Eve and not had the other person get it for three hours? That's because the network is overloaded. Now imagine that at that moment when everything is already congested, part of the network goes offline for upgrade works.

Not a happy thought, right? Whenever we work on a network, parts of it have to go offline. The Australian government decreed that that's a no-go over the holidays and implemented the telco embargo period. During this time, only specific maintenance works can be performed. Nothing else. Basically, all telcos shut down, barring a skeleton crew, during this time. This year, the embargo begins on December 14 and runs until January 7.

And that's why we're bang on schedule, but also two weeks behind. The contracts were signed before anyone noticed the change, and although Jimmy, legal, and the CEO have repeatedly pointed out that it was a mistake and that the original timeline that was agreed to can still be met, the client is being a bastard about it—because if we don't meet the deadline, we have to pay penalties. Considering how much this project is costing them, the thought of getting even a little bit of that back must have them salivating.

Jimmy's priority right now is getting an extra two weeks' work out of the teams in the eastern states, but my priority is getting Western Australia, South Australia, and the Northern Territory (WASANT) back on budget. Those three states, under the watchful eye of project manager Paul Hanks, will meet the earlier deadline (barring catastrophe, knock on wood).

Paul Hanks.

My biggest challenge.

I've never met Paul before—he's spent the last seven years working in Bangladesh, and our paths didn't cross before that—but I've heard about him. He's a straight-down-the-line blokey bloke who takes shit from no one, but has the respect, if not liking, of everyone who works for him. Or so I'm told. I still haven't spoken to him, because he *won't take my calls.*

On my second day in this job, I sat down with Mae, the most senior of the RAs on my team, for a candid update. When the conversation turned to WASANT and Paul Hanks, she made a sound that could have been a sob, a groan, or a combination of the two.

"I take it Paul's going to cause us problems?" I asked her dryly, and she made the sound again.

"If you can get Paul to even acknowledge your existence, you'll be doing a thousand times better than any of us did." She sighed and scrunched up her face. "I can't even blame him. He was trying to do the right thing from the beginning. As soon as word got out that the project was two weeks behind before we even started, Paul called Dipshit"

—the nickname pretty much sums up how the team feels about their former boss—"to get things cracking. He'd worked out a plan that would keep his sites on the revised schedule, but he needed an additional 5 percent of resources."

I raised my brows. "Really? Only five?" In the grand scheme of a project like this, 5 percent is nothing. Dipshit should have sent him a case of beer and wept in gratitude.

Mae nodded. "Yeah. You know my desk is next to yours, right? And Dipshit always used to put his phone on speaker, which, I mean...." We share a look. Nothing is more inconsiderate than putting your phone on speaker in an open-plan office. "So I basically heard the whole convo. He told Paul that *he* was the resource manager and *he* would 'determine the solution.'"

"Shit," I muttered. No wonder Paul didn't like resource management.

"Oh, that wasn't the worst part. Paul was actually pretty good about that bit. He didn't sound happy, but he agreed and said he'd wait for a call."

I already knew that Dipshit was a complete wanker, but this was getting ridiculous. "Do I want to know the rest?" I asked.

Mae grinned. "Probably not, but you need to. Paul waited two days, called again, was given the runaround again, waited two more days, called again, and I kid you not, Dipshit told him that he needed to be patient. So Paul lost it. Told Dipshit to fuck himself with a cactus," she said gleefully, and I laughed so hard I nearly choked. "Despite our best efforts, he's been doing his own resourcing since. He won't take any calls from anyone in the resource management department."

Since Mae's revelations that day, I've put a lot of

thought into the situation. I don't really blame Paul for not wanting to talk to us, and since his solution actually worked and his sites are the only ones on schedule, normally I'd let him nurse his grudge and get on with it. *But...* Paul's the biggest culprit of those using non-approved agencies to get bodies on site, and he's blown the budget out obscenely.

"If I can get the rest of the rollout on track to meet the deadline, it won't be a problem," Jimmy explained to me with a somewhat desperate undertone during our initial meeting. "The penalties at this stage are about the same as what Paul's spent, give or take a hundred thousand or so, but it looks a lot worse for us to miss the first deadline than to overspend the budget temporarily. And you know if we miss the first deadline, we're not likely to make the others, so there will be more penalties. Spending a bit more now to save later is something I can sell to the board. But if we miss the deadline *and* we're this far overbudget, I'll be out, and whoever they replace me with will be scrambling to look like he's getting somewhere, which means he'll probably replace half the PMs."

"Changing PMs at that stage would just fuck everything up," I mused, studying the schedule on the screen. "But yeah. He'd have to."

So Jimmy and I agreed that he'd keep his focus on the project itself and let me worry about getting the resourcing budget under control. Of course, there's no way I can reduce expenditure enough before the end of the year, but I can plug the holes and show a decrease in spending, plus projections of how that will continue to improve. And if I can get Paul Hanks to talk to me, we can adapt his strategy for application in the other states.

Now, I make sure my team's aware of what's needed

this week and send them back to their desks. I'm all but certain that I'll be out of the office for a few days. The situation in WASANT needs to be resolved.

I'm really thrilled with the solution I've come up with. The contractors Paul hired are all skilled and experienced, and *we're actually going to need them* in the next phase of the project. He skimmed the cream when he was recruiting, and no way do I want to piss these guys off by replacing them with other contractors who aren't as good but are cheaper. Like I said, we're going to need them next year, and I want them leaping at the chance to come back. We bring on contractors when our employee resources are assigned to other projects, but if an employee with the relevant skills and experience is freed up, the contractor is almost always let go. It's cheaper to use an employee, better for company morale, and given the kind confidential design work involved, more secure. Contractors know that, and while they don't necessarily love it, they're cool with it. They know they're an essential part of the industry and that they'll likely be back working on a project soon.

No way would they stand for being replaced by other contractors, though. And we can't end their contract through the expensive agency and rehire through a preferred one—that would cause all sorts of contractual legal shit with the agencies. So you can see the bind I was in, *am still in* until I manage to get it sorted out. Like I said, I have a solution—I just have to apply it. And for that, I need Paul Hanks.

I've been on this project for over five weeks, and I still haven't spoken to Paul. Well, that's not strictly true. I sit in on the weekly PM status meetings, and three times I've asked him at the end of the meeting if he'll stay on the line for a few minutes. He agrees, and then as soon as Jimmy leaves the room and all the other PMs have disconnected, makes an excuse and hangs up. His poor project administrator was almost in tears the last time I called her to schedule a teleconference with him. Probably because she knew he was going to cancel at the last minute like he had the previous four times and leave her to break it to me.

Last week, I decided to get around the whole won't-take-my-calls thing by sending him a very detailed email laying out my plan. But the bastard hasn't even opened the damn thing—I'm still waiting for a read receipt.

This leaves me with two options: I either go to Jimmy, explain everything that's happened, and let him solve my problems by reaming out Paul—which is going to make me look like I can't handle the situation *and* earn me an enemy —or I get sneaky.

Guess what I've decided on?

Step one: I call Rachel, Paul's project administrator, and ask her to book thirty minutes of his time for a call with me for tomorrow.

"Um, okay," she concedes. "But, Duncan, you know it'll be a miracle if he doesn't cancel. Maybe I should block the time out but not put what it's for? If we're lucky, he won't notice until you actually call, and you might be able to keep him on the line." She sounds doubtful.

"Nope," I say cheerfully. "Let's not piss him off before we even begin. He'll be in the office, yeah? I mean, I won't have to track him down on some remote site?" It's a really stupid question for a teleconference, because we work for a telco.

"Yeah." Rachel seems not to notice how weird the question is. "He's got a site meeting late in the afternoon, but he'll be in the office until noon."

Perfect.

Step two: book a flight to Perth for this evening. Because of the time difference, I could get the first flight out tomorrow and still make it in time for our ten thirty appointment, but I'm not risking that the plane might be delayed, or traffic from the airport might hold me up. I *will* be there to make sure Paul can't escape me. A seven o'clock flight tonight will give me time—just—to get to the airport straight from work. The best part about working for a telco is that they go out of their way to make sure employees can work from literally anywhere. Hot-desking is revered by upper management.

Step three: make sure my plan is clear, concise, and that I have all the materials I need to support it—and implement it as soon as Paul agrees. Which he will. He might hate all resource managers with the fire of a thousand suns because of Dipshit, but he's a top project manager and, according to word around the office, a decent bloke. He knows he's overbudget, and it's gotta be rankling.

All I need is some of his time.

I deliberately loiter in a coffee shop across the street from the Perth office. I don't want to arrive early and give Paul time to come up with an escape plan, but there was no way I was risking being late. I take the time to go over my plan again, checking it for any flaw that might have sneaked past my and Krista's eagle eyes.

There aren't any. But it's a great opportunity to implant every detail in my brain while sucking back a coffee.

The shop is only moderately busy—we're well past the I-just-arrived-at-work-and-desperately-need-a-coffee rush, and not quite at the midmorning coffee break rush.

There are a few small groups efficiently combining coffee with a meeting at the tables, and a couple of other loners like me sitting in armchairs, hunched over laptops, but voices are low and there's not a lot of ambient noise.

So the strident ring of the shop phone gets my attention, and I'm still only half-focused a minute later when one of the staff calls to another, "Paul's on his way—make his usual, will you?"

There are a lot of Pauls in the world. In fact, there are probably a lot of Pauls currently within a one-block radius. But a guy who phones in his coffee order when he's on his way is either superefficient or an asshole, and Paul Hanks has been described as both. Plus, this place is the closest to our Perth office, so it makes sense that he'd use it. And the timing is about right for a break before his meeting with me.

I slouch down a little in my seat. There's no reason to think he knows what I look like, but it feels like the done thing. I mean, if you're potentially spying on someone, you're supposed to be all sneaky, right?

Never mind.

I'm just wondering if maybe I've been watching too many police procedural TV shows when the door to the street opens and a man walks in.

Remember, I've never actually met Paul Hanks before. I've seen a picture of him, though—it was from a company party a couple of years ago, in profile, and not terribly clear. But it's enough for me to recognise him and to marvel at what the picture *didn't* show.

He's fucking huge.

Tall, yes—about six-three, although it's hard to judge with me sitting down. But it's more that he's built like a brick shithouse. Broad across the shoulders, with a tank for a torso. He's just *solid*. I can't tell with how he's dressed—chinos and a long-sleeved shirt—if that solid is muscle or fat, but whatever it is, it's imposing. His face is average—attractive enough, although he'd never win any awards for his looks—and he has a ruddy complexion. His hair is dark blond, in an all-over messy style that makes me think he usually has it quite short and it's just overgrown.

But the most important detail is his presence. Seriously. He walks in, and it's like the room is full to bursting. I can't stop staring. He has serious charisma, but not of the charming variety. It's more like a force of nature, blasting through all that stands in its way.

In just a few strides, he's at the counter and accepting the paper cup offered to him.

"Hey, Paul," the young man behind the register says as he rings up the sale. "How's the morning?"

"Not as bad as it could be," he replies, handing over some cash. His voice is deep enough to stir something carnal in me—I've always been a sucker for a deep voice. I shift slightly, reminding myself that I'm not here for that, that I cannot jeopardise my one chance to get him on side by letting my sexual urges get in the way.

He's not even that good-looking. It's a stupid, petty attempt to convince myself, even if it is true. I've met better-looking guys—hell, one of my exes was so fucking hot that people on the street would turn to watch him walk past. Just because Paul is built, has an amazing voice, and can't stand me (we've talked about how I love a challenge, right?) doesn't mean I should think of him that way.

And yes, he's gay. I'm not engaging in pointless fantasy here. Well, I am, but not for that reason. Paul being gay is one of the worst-kept secrets in our incestuous, gossipy industry. He managed to keep it under wraps when he was a site engineer, but once he transitioned to mostly working in the office, it came out—no pun intended. He doesn't advertise, but enough people know that it's not a secret. He's been in the industry long enough, and earned the respect of enough people, that it's not an issue. From what I've heard, there's occasionally some fuckwit on a site who tries to make something of it, but they get shouted down pretty quick.

Paul finishes his transaction and leaves, and I take my first real breath since he walked in.

Okay. It's go time.

four

I STRIDE into the reception of the Perth office and smile at the woman behind the desk. "Hi, I'm Duncan Witten from the Melbourne office. How's your day been?"

She returns the smile as she slides the visitor log to me, and I pass her my company ID. "Good, thanks. Are you here to see anyone in particular, or just hot-desking?" She enters my ID number on her keyboard and pulls out a visitor tag so I can get through the security gate. I scrawl my details into the log.

"Paul Hanks, but he doesn't know it yet. Can you point me toward Rachel Johns's desk?" I take back my ID plus the visitor tag and hang both around my neck. With wide eyes, she gives me directions, and I flash another smile before swiping myself through the gate and making my way through the maze of desks.

I hear him before I see him. He's standing next to a pretty young woman with dark hair, and he sounds exasperated.

"—not going to get into trouble for this, Rachel. You're doing it on my order. Just cancel the damn teleconference."

To give Rachel her due, she seems more annoyed than worried that she'll get into trouble. "Why can't you just take the call? The amount of time you've spent dodging him over the past month adds up to way more than a half-hour phone call. Just listen to what he has to say. It's damn embarrassing to have to cancel all the time."

Paul groans. "Why are you embarrassed? The guy's not an idiot, he knows it's all on me, and I'm not embarrassed. Just tell him a site emergency came up. He won't believe it, but what can he do?"

"While I'm thrilled you don't think I'm an idiot, what I can do is turn up in person for our meeting."

They both turn to look at me, and I beam at them.

"Hey, you must be Rachel. I'm Duncan Witten." I offer her my hand. She picks her jaw up off the floor and shakes it.

"Hi," she breathes, eyes wide. She darts a sideways glance at Paul, and a tiny smile sneaks onto her face. "Uh, it's great to meet you in person. Let me book a meeting room for you."

"Thanks." I turn to Paul as she sits at a desk—hers, presumably—and I stick out my hand. "Nice to meet you, Paul."

He hesitates for so long that I begin to think he's actually going to refuse to shake hands, but then he steps up and takes my hand. His is warm and large, and that tiny bit of desire I pushed down earlier revives itself. I ignore it.

"Did I know you were coming out?" he asks, and then must realise how rude he sounds. "I mean, if I'd known, I would have made sure the day was clear." He makes a face and shakes his head. "Yeah, that's a lie. Sorry, mate, but I just don't have time for you. Like you heard, I've got to get out for a site visit."

Well, I've got to give him points for bluntness. And stubbornness.

"That's not until this afternoon," Rachel pipes up helpfully, and I could kiss her.

Paul glares. It's pretty intimidating.

Rachel smiles at him.

"It was," he says through gritted teeth, "but I had a call this morning and I need to go out earlier."

"That's okay," I assure him, and then just as his face relaxes, I add, "I'll come with you."

Rachel laughs. Actually laughs. Other people are starting to pay attention, sneaking glances and surreptitiously straining to hear. The downside of an open-plan office.

Paul works hard to keep his face from showing how much he hates that idea. He's unsuccessful. "Constipated" would be a good word to describe his expression.

"You haven't had the site safety induction."

Really? That's the best he can come up with? Pffft. I mean, that's so easily overcome by just waiting in the car when he gets to the site, but as it happens...

"Sure I have." I make a point of always doing company safety inductions for rural sites, just in case I need to unexpectedly visit. As a rule, my job doesn't require me to go on site—I know RMs who've never left head office before—but I've found I get better results from the line if I occasionally let them see my face. There's usually an additional safety induction that's specific to each site, but if you've done the company one, the extra only takes about fifteen minutes. "My certification is on the intranet register."

He narrows his eyes. "You don't have any PPE."

I give him my sunniest smile. "I'm sure they have spare on site."

This leaves him in a quandary. If he says no, there's no extra PPE—personal protective equipment—on site, he's dumping the site supervisor in a pile of shit. Company policy is to keep extra PPE on every site for visitors. Nobody is allowed on a site without PPE, no exceptions, and the best way to ensure this rule is endorsed is to have gear available.

If he says yes, though, then there's really nothing stopping me from going with him to the site.

"I'm not going to be back until after hours," he tries. "You'll miss your flight." He's squared his shoulders, arms hanging loosely by his sides—a battle stance, ready for anything. Is it wrong that I find that both utterly adorable and incredibly sexy?

"Oh, I don't have a return flight booked. I'm here for as long as it takes to get things done." It's a challenge. A grudging respect flashes in his gaze for a split second, then it's gone and he's scowling again.

"Fine. But no whining. I'm leaving in fifteen minutes. Get yourself a sandwich or something if you're going to want lunch, because I'm not stopping." He stomps away— well, not really, but his stride definitely conveys his displeasure.

I look to Rachel, who has a delighted grin on her face and the company chat app open on her laptop. No doubt news of this confrontation will travel like wildfire. "If I run out to get food, is he likely to leave without me?"

She nods. "Probably. Hang on. I brought lunch from home today. You can take that, and I'll buy something." She rummages in a canvas bag under her desk and comes out with two wrapped sandwiches and an apple. I give her some money to cover lunch and stash the food in my laptop bag.

"You're an angel. Anything I should know before I get in a car with him?" I'm mostly kidding, but given Paul's distinctly unenthusiastic response to my presence, part of me is serious.

She laughs. "You'll be fine. Paul can be a real dick sometimes, but he's still a great guy. By the time you're out of the city, he'll be over it."

I hope she's right.

I keep my mouth shut for the first part of the drive. Paul looked grumpy as hell when he came back from wherever and packed up his laptop and shit, so I followed him out to his car without saying anything to further antagonise him. After all, I need him to be on my side, not plotting to dump me by the side of the highway. He takes a couple of calls—it's the lot in life of a project manager to be surgically attached to a phone—but we're headed northeast out of Perth on Toodyay Road before I speak up. I'm mentally picturing the rollout map and how far along Paul's team is with the sites, trying to narrow down which one we could be headed for.

Finally, I just ask. It's as good a way to begin conversation as any, right?

"Which site are we headed to?"

He doesn't take his eyes off the road, but answers readily enough. "Beacon."

The map in my mind's eye isn't great, but I made a point of familiarising myself with Paul's sites and progress before coming to Perth, so I have a decent idea of where we're going. If I'm remembering right, the Beacon site is out towards the edge of the "blanket" coverage area. Further north and east of there, network coverage will be confined to corridors along the highways and patches where there's denser population. I'm not sure exactly how long the drive will be, but I figure about three or four hours each way, and we're only forty-five minutes in.

Perfect.

"We could sit in silence the whole way, but that would defeat the purpose of me being here, so I'm going to talk. You can pretend not to listen if you like." I really hope he doesn't take me up on that. I said it more to break the ice than anything else, but I regretted it the second it came out of my mouth.

I hurry on. "First up, I want to apologise on behalf of all resource managers everywhere for the dipshit you had to deal with before." Not strictly professional, but hey. "I can't tell you how much crap he left us to wade through, and how thankful I am that you told him to get fucked and sorted out your own resourcing." That's laying it on a little thick, but none of it's untrue.

"I didn't tell him to get fucked," Paul corrects, and I seize on the opportunity to make a connection.

"Sorry, yeah, it was 'go fuck yourself with a cactus,' right?"

A smile tugs at his mouth. It doesn't quite develop, but the self-satisfied expression on his profile says it all.

"You heard about that, huh?"

I chuckle, not bothering to try and stifle it. "It's made the rounds of the office. Dipshit made a formal complaint, but somehow the paperwork still hasn't been lodged with HR. It just keeps getting emailed from person to person." Nobody is going to lodge that paperwork. It would take a much more serious and offensive insult between equals than "fuck yourself" for more than a verbal reprimand.

When asked, Jimmy solemnly swears that he spoke severely to Paul about use of inappropriate language in the workplace. I'd bet everything I own that no such conversation ever took place.

"Well, the guy pissed me off."

"Me too, and I never met him. He left me a real shit pile to clean up, and it doesn't help that he burned as many bridges as he could for the department."

Paul says nothing for ages, and I'm just beginning to wonder if I'll have to dive in cold when he glances over. "So I'm not the only one who preferred to do my own resourcing than deal with him?"

"No," I admit. "Although you're the only one who's actually done a halfway decent job of it." It might seem like flattery, but it's not. None of the other regions are in as good a place as his is.

"Only halfway? Mine is the only region that's on target, and that's because I did my own resourcing."

"You're massively overbudget," I remind him.

He pulls a face. "I know. It's temporary. The contracts are for stage one only, and as soon as they're up, I'll negotiate better rates for stage two." He shoots me another glance. "So I have it under control, and you don't need to be here after all."

In other words, *I don't need you, fuck off.*

Um, no.

"As thrilling as it is to know that you've looked ahead, there are a couple of problems with your plan." I wince. *Dial down the snark, Dunc.* "To begin with, it hinges on you still being in charge of the region for stage two."

Yeah. I didn't do so great on dialling down the snark.

He whips his head around and pins me with a glare. I

get the feeling that I'm lucky he's driving and doesn't have a free hand to deck me with. "Is that a threat?"

I raise my hands, palms out. "Hell, no. It wouldn't be up to me. But if Jimmy can't get Vic/Tas, NSW, and QLD across the line in time, we're going to be up for penalties in addition to the budget overspend. He'll be out, and the entire project management team will go up for review. You're massively overbudget, Paul," I repeat. "The board and the paper pushers who do the review aren't going to care that you did it to correct someone else's mistake. They're not going to listen to promises that it can be fixed in the next stage unless you can show them it's already in train. And the fact is, the agencies will hold you hostage. They're going to drag their feet on giving you a better rate. You need to have the contractor agreements for stage two in place before stage one is complete, and they won't do that if you're negotiating rates. The project will come to a standstill while you're battling it out with them, and you'll lose the time you so expensively made up in stage one." There's no physical break between stages—stage one ends one day, and stage two begins the next. "Not to mention the money you'll be spending over the next six weeks while stage one is being completed."

Silence falls again while he thinks that over. I don't think any of that is news to him. Honestly, knowing what I do about him, I'll bet he's fully aware of everything I've said, knows he's painted himself into a corner, and is hanging on by his fingertips, hoping everything works out.

"I reckon you think you've got a solution."

It's not a question, but I treat it as one. "Yes. I— *We* can't do anything about the other regions. That's Jimmy's problem, although later I want to talk about how you implemented your resourcing plan and see if any of it can be applied elsewhere or if it's too late. But we can cut costs here and show that you're getting expenditure under control before stage one ends. The board would see that as a bonus if we meet the deadline, and if we don't, it's probably the only thing that will save your and Jimmy's jobs." I study his profile, but he's keeping his expression neutral.

Please see the sense in what I'm saying.

"How?"

"How can we cut costs? Well, the easiest way would be to get cheaper agency rates, but as you know, that's not going to happen until the contracts are up. So we need to replace the contractors with company employees."

"Oh, is that all?" he scoffs. "Look, mate, you had me going there for a bit, but if you're just here to make yourself look good, don't waste my fucking time. There're no company employees available. I've tried that; I've *been trying that* for six months. The line managers won't take my calls anymore, I've rung them so often."

"No, there's no one available here in Australia. But it's a global company, Paul. As RM, I have access to company employees around the world."

He shakes his head. "I thought of that, but getting work visas for them is a bitch. The government is trying to keep as much work in the hands of Aussies as possible. By the time you get the visas through, stage one will be over."

I grin, because this is my trump card. "New Zealanders don't need special visas to work here."

He scoffs again. "The team in New Zealand is small. There's no way they'll have enough people free to help us out. You'll get one or two blokes, five at the maximum." He glances at me again. "Nice try, though. You've clearly spent more time thinking about this than the other guy."

"More than you, too," I inform him. "New Zealand just

finished a major rollout of their own. Nothing on this scale, but significant enough."

"I know," he says, exasperated. "I do work in this industry. I know all the major rollouts going on around the world."

"Right," I agree. "So you know that they planned to go right from that project into another one, and that it fell through at the last second."

"Stop fucking around and get to the fucking point," he demands. "I don't have time to play word games with you."

Since we're stuck in the car together for the next couple hours, it seems like he does, but I stop myself from pointing that out.

"The point is, when the New Zealand resourcing team was planning for the rollout that just finished, they thought they'd have back-to-back projects spanning a four-year period, crunched the numbers, and decided it would be cheaper and more efficient to bring on permanent employees than contractors. When this latest project fell through, negotiations were already underway for another project to commence in February, so when the rollout wrapped up last month, rather than make anyone redundant only to have to bring on contractors later, they decided to wear the cost of having teams idle until the new rollout begins."

"What? *What?*" There's an edge in his voice that sounds a lot like hope.

"They have a team literally sitting around telling fart jokes while their cost centre bleeds. I had a chat with resourcing and the line manager over there, and they just about wept tears of joy when I said I needed them. This is pure dumb luck," I admit, because it is. The coincidence of a whole team being available right when we need them is incalculable.

"You're telling me the *entire* team that just did the rollout in New Zealand is available to come over and finish out stage one for us?" He pauses, and I can almost hear him doing the calculations. "They've got, what, twenty-five, thirty guys?"

"Thirty-four," I correct. It's nowhere near the number we're using across the country, because New Zealand is a helluva lot smaller than Australia, but Paul's got over seventy contractors working across his region alone, and this will enable us to replace nearly half of them. "The big benefit is that the New Zealand dollar is worth less than ours, so their rate is less than what we'd have to pay to an Aussie team. Some of that is eaten up by the cost of getting them over here, but because your rural sites already budget for accommodation and expenses, it still works out better for us—a lot better." I can't resist adding, "I laid out the exact figures in the email I sent you last week." If he'd opened it, we could have those guys here right now instead of just discussing it.

He huffs, then says grudgingly, "I guess I should have read the damn thing, then. Jimmy seen these numbers?"

I'm not sure how to take that. It feels an awful lot like he doesn't trust me. *Patience, Dunc. When this is all done, you can tell him exactly how you feel.*

"He has. We talked about using the NZ team to speed up work in one of the east coast states, but if we need to add accommodation and a per diem to their rate, it's no longer a bargain, so we can only really put them to good use on rural sites. Since you have the most rural sites, Jimmy agreed that I could offer them to you." *And you would be an idiot to refuse.*

"When can you get them out?"

I hold back my victorious grin. "They can be ready to start work Monday."

He takes his eyes off the road to give me a surprised look. "So soon?"

I shrug. "Well, if you didn't want them, I knew we could use them on the sites in far north Queensland. I basically told them to be ready to fly out this weekend—they're just waiting to hear where to." Slyly, I add, "Dean Grech offered me a case of beer if I 'forgot' to give you first right of refusal." Dean is the PM in charge of the Queensland roll-out, an always happy, florid-faced man with a full white beard who earned the nickname of Santa—for obvious reasons.

"No fucking way," Paul declares immediately. "Tell 'em to fly into Perth. I'll get Rachel to organize a hotel for Sunday night, and Monday we'll get them out to the sites. Is the safety induction the same in New Zealand as here?"

I already have my phone in my hand, bringing up the contact for the New Zealand line manager. "Mostly, but there are enough differences that I had them do the Aussie one as well. It's the only time I've ever seen anyone happy to do a safety induction, so I reckon they're getting bored with trying to get around the company firewall to play online poker." The call connects, and I spend a couple minutes confirming the details and listening to Gary—the manager—thank me for lining up this work. Paul is also on the phone, talking to Rachel, and interrupts me at one point to ask for Gary's contact details. I give them to him, then tell Gary that Rachel will be in touch. We both end our calls at about the same time.

"Rachel wanted to know what to do about the contractors and the agencies. I told her you'd handle it." It's a challenge, but one I'm more than up for—after all, dealing with the agencies is part of my job.

"No worries. I need a list of who you'll be replacing. Do you want a word with the blokes before I let them know?"

"Yeah. I'll shoot round a message, and Rachel will get you that list today. We want this lot back for stage two, yeah."

I nod, even though he's telling me, not asking. "Definitely. We can have the New Zealanders until embargo, and then bring them back for a couple weeks in Jan if we need them, but starting Feb, they'll either have their own project to worry about or they'll be made redundant." I pause and bite my lip. "If their project falls through, we could keep them longer. As long as they're allocated to a project and billing, that shouldn't be a problem. But we won't know for sure until mid-December, so it's safer to plan for them to be gone."

He grunts. "You got a plan for dealing with the agencies?"

I sneak a peek at him. He looks less tense now. I'm going to say that's partly because he's realised I'm not the devil incarnate, and partly because we've just reduced his resource expenditure by literally thousands of dollars per day.

"I do," I answer. "Our three preferred agencies in Perth have already been given a heads-up about recruitment for stage two. Barring catastrophe, your region will be commencing those works as soon as embargo ends, even if the other states don't make the deadline and run behind. So it's not unreasonable to begin recruitment now. I'll tell the guys we're letting go who they should get in touch with if they want to come back onto the project, and I'll tell the agencies that no interview is required for those guys. Just let me know if there's anyone you don't want back," I tack on, and he shakes his head.

"We haven't had problems with anyone lately. I had to replace a few a couple months back, two for slacking and one for theft, but the rest seem to be solid."

"Good." It really is—there's a lot of autonomy on rural sites, and things like theft can easily become problems if the site supervisor and PM don't keep a sharp eye out. "The agencies you're currently using aren't going to be offered the opportunity to recruit for stage two. I was a bit concerned that I'd have to negotiate with them, but since you so wisely limited their contracts to stage one"—I shoot him a teasing glance and see his lips twitch—"I don't have to. We're not under any contractual obligation to continue working with them. I just need to make sure all the guys we're keeping on know that if they want to continue with stage two, they need to get in touch with our preferred agencies for new contracts once their current ones end. It's a bit dodgy, since the original agencies did all the recruitment work to source these guys, but they've been screwing us all year and so now I'm going to screw them."

He laughs.

Oh.

My.

God.

That laugh.

Seriously.

No joke, I go half hard just listening to him laugh. It's... ungh. I have no words.

So I'm sitting in the passenger seat, turned on, unable to adjust myself for fear of drawing his attention to my semi, listening to him laugh and desperately wanting to lick the long, muscled line of his throat. Since the guy couldn't stand me just a couple hours ago—who am I kidding? He still couldn't stand me twenty minutes ago—and is only just beginning to warm up, it's unlikely he'll go for it if I suggest he pulls off the road so I can suck his dick.

Plus, you know. Unprofessional. Don't shit where you work. Too old for casual sex—although seriously, who made up that rule? Probably some jackass who could only get laid if he had a serious boyfriend.

"Yeah," I croak, desperate to distract myself. "Uh, so mostly all I have to do is spread the word around the sites. If you're okay with it, I'll send an email to the site supervisors and have them mention it in morning briefing."

"Send me the details," he says, and oh, hell, I swear his voice is an octave or two deeper. "I'll send the email to the sites and cc you. Some of the site guys can be weird about head office."

A bit of my composure comes back. *Awwww, how sweet! I'm getting him on side.* He doesn't need to worry, though —I had a look at the list of his site supervisors, and I've worked on projects with about two thirds of them before. I'm confident I can get their buy-in on anything I try to sell. But I'm not going to argue with him if he's trying to help. "Sure."

My phone rings in my hand, startling me—and drawing Paul's attention briefly to my lap. The car swerves slightly.

Fuck. Fuck fuck fuck. He saw. He had to have. There's really no way he could have missed it. The question is, does he think I'm some kind of freak who gets turned on talking about resource planning, or does he know I'm attracted to him?

Attracted to him. It sounds so mild. So neat and tidy. The truth is nothing like that. It's desperate and hot and *hard*, damn it.

I glance at my traitorous phone. "It's Jimmy," I manage to say, sounding strangled *because I don't know what he's thinking.* I answer the call.

"Dunc, your team said you're in Perth. What the hell? Is something wrong?" He sounds stressed out of his mind, and I'm so glad I don't have to tell him about the problems I was having with Paul.

"Nope, nothing wrong. Paul and I needed to sort out some details, and I figured it would be easier if I hot-desked out here for a few days. The New Zealand guys start Monday, and I've got about fifteen other company employees from various countries who're interested in working in Aus for a while. I'm looking into how quick I can push through their visas." Paul glances sharply my way, but I ignore it. Even if he doesn't want them, we can use them elsewhere on the project. Dean Grech would kiss my feet if I could get him more hands on deck with knowledge of the company's proprietary network designs, which contractors don't have.

"Oh, good," Jimmy says, audibly relieved. "Listen, can you put out the word with your agency contacts? Mike Bates has promised me that with another ten guys, he can meet the deadline in Vic. He needs them now, though."

"No worries," I assure him breezily, my mind racing. Another ten qualified, experienced rollout engineers ASAP? Fuck. "Let me make some calls and I'll give you an update by COB." Oh, shit. WA is three hours behind Melbourne at this time of year. I glance at the dash clock. "Or first thing tomorrow," I amend. It's already mid-afternoon in Melbourne, and my agency contacts can only do so much.

Jimmy agrees and disconnects, and I shoot off a quick text to Mike, asking him to wander across the office to my team and let them know exactly what skill sets he wants in the new guys. I get a thumbs-up emoji back, and then flick through my contacts. "Sorry, gotta make some calls," I mumble to Paul. I can't even look at him, especially since my erection isn't completely gone. I mean, I'm not at full salute, but if you look, it's noticeable.

I manage to get through the calls to our preferred agencies in Victoria, telling them I need the resources ASAP and that my team has the details, and I can pretty much hear the gritted teeth as they assure me they'll do what they can. I make another call to Mae on my team and ask her to take a wander through the office and chat up some of the engineers, see if anyone knows anyone who might be interested. Leave no stone unturned, and all that.

But then there's nobody else to call. I mean, there is—there are always calls to make—but nothing that's urgent, nothing that would justify being so rude as to make a call while in someone else's company.

Nothing that can shield me from having to talk to Paul again. Hear his fabulous voice and remember what it sounds like laughing.

Oh, fuck me, just the thought is turning me on!

Nope. No way. This is not happening.

"Sorry about that," I say as breezily as I can, dropping my phone in my lap. Hopefully it'll help to hide the situation in my pants. I grit my teeth and try to think about the most disgusting things I've ever encountered in office fridges.

He clears his throat. "No worries." Is it just me, or does his voice sound a bit strained? "So, ah, you're looking at international teams?"

"Yes." I stare through the windshield and keep my voice as normal as possible. I've been attracted—there's that lovely, safe word again—to colleagues before. Who hasn't?

Doesn't mean I have to act on it, right? "Not specifically for your sites, though. We need the extra hands, especially anyone who's already rolled out our IP on a big project."

"Right." Cue awkward silence.

Now what? I was making genuine headway, and my stupid dick ruined it. I'm going to be working with this guy for the next two years, and sure, maybe we'll be in offices across the country from each other, but we'll likely be in contact every day in some form or another. Project resourcing is ever-changing, and a strong relationship between PM and RM is essential. Otherwise you get problems like the one I'm currently trying to solve.

So do I apologise? Make a joke? Assure him it's not personal? At least I know he's not homophobic—that's pretty much the only way this could be worse.

I decide to acknowledge it but play it off as trivial.

"Nothing like a spirited victory to get the blood pumping," I say, and as soon as the words are out of my mouth, I groan and bury my face in my hands, because what. The. *Fuck?*

I mean... what the fuck?

Really. What?

I'm trying to decide if it would be completely insane or just a little bit insane to throw myself from a vehicle moving at 110 kilometres per hour when a small part of my brain registers a sound.

Laughter, to be precise.

Gut-busting laughter.

Slowly, I ease my hands down from my face and sneak a sideways peek at him. He's laughing so hard that I'm a little worried he's going to drive off the road. I focus on that in an attempt to *not* get turned on again. (Spoiler: I fail.)

"I'd be offended that you're laughing at me, but I

deserve it. When I'm past the mortification I'm feeling right now, I'll probably laugh too."

He sobers enough to look over at me, and God, his *face*. The grin spread across it transforms him. He was vaguely good-looking before, but now I just want to bite him all over. While he's laughing.

Okay, maybe not. That would be too weird. While he's talking? Yeah. While he's giving me orders in that sinful voice....

This is not helping the situation in my pants.

I take a deep breath, then let it out. "So... I hope I haven't offended you."

The last of his chuckles die down, and he swipes his tears of laughter from his eyes. Because only I could turn an erection into a way to make a guy laugh so hard he cries. "Nah, mate. She's all good."

I smile weakly. "Thanks." What else can I say? Even if I'm still as much in the dark as I was before. Does he know I'm turned on by him, or does he think it's some weird other thing? I mean, don't get me wrong, either way I'm chuffed that he knows I can get it up with so little encouragement—I *am* forty-one, after all, not seventeen—but I still have no idea if he would welcome a come-on or not.

Don't shit where you eat, Dunc, remember?

five

PAUL PARKS the car in front of the site office. We're not far from the town of Beacon, and this is the current base for works along this arm of the rollout. The "site" looks like a village of shipping containers. They're not actually shipping containers, just prefab, transportable "buildings" for use as offices and accommodation on temporary sites like this—called dongas, in case you were wondering. To be honest, I can't imagine much that I'd dislike more than living in the middle of nowhere in a metal box, even if it is temporary, but some of these guys go from project to project and don't take any of their leave time.

"I shouldn't need to be too long," Paul promises as we get out and head toward the site office. "I could have handled this meeting over the phone, but it's been a while since I visited this site and I like to be visible."

"No worries," I assure him. "It's good for me to get out to sites, and I've got plenty to keep me busy."

We walk into the office, and a young man I assume is the site administrator looks up from a desk and grins. "Hey, Paul. He's waiting for you. Who's this?"

Did I mention that sometimes the rural site employees can get a little blunt? Nobody in the city offices would ever just ask straight out like that. Gotta admit, it's one of the things I miss about living out bush.

One of the very few things.

I hold out a hand to him. "Duncan Witten, from Resource Management." Some days it feels like all I do is introduce myself.

He shakes my hand. "Ooh, we in trouble?" He cackles, and I bite back a laugh of my own. "Dom Jones."

"What the fuck's goin' on out here?"

I turn toward the short hallway leading to the rest of the donga and see a familiar face. He recognises me at the same time, and a grin breaks out on his weathered, deeply tanned face. "Dunc Witten, you bastard! They stuck you with this sorry mess, did they?" He comes forward to shake my hand and slap me on the back. I grin and slap him back.

"Begged me to come and fix you all up," I tell him. "Whatcha doing this far south, Brian?" I've worked with Brian before several times. He was one of the guys on the first site I ever visited, about fifteen years ago.

"Paulie here brought me down a couple months back to speed this lot along. That's the trouble with being good at your fucking job—you gotta fix things when other people fuck theirs up." I say nothing, because... well, I'm here, aren't I? "Come on back and get a coffee." I follow him, and Paul falls into step with me.

"So you two know each other?" he says, sounding calm and maybe a little curious. Should I have told him there was a good chance this would happen? I didn't because... what if we'd arrived and the site manager had been a stranger? Then it would have looked like I was trying to big-note myself.

Brian answers before I can.

"Sure, known Dunc for years, since he was a baby resource manager. Came out to a site and had a huge blue with the supervisor, called him an incompetent asshole to his face in front of the whole site."

I wince. I was hoping we could avoid that bit, but it seems that story never gets old.

"What?" Paul asks incredulously, turning to me as we go into the tiny break room-slash-kitchenette.

"It wasn't exactly like that," I protest, and when Brian snorts, "well, okay, maybe it was. But it was an accident." This day is not doing a lot to convince Paul I'm a competent, professional RM. You know, what with the erection and the story about me calling colleagues assholes.

"You accidentally called him an incompetent asshole in front of the whole site?"

Yeah. I can't blame him for sounding dubious.

"I didn't mean for the whole site to hear," I explain. "We were walking into a room, and I didn't know everyone was waiting in there for morning briefing. And the acoustics were really good." Like, shockingly good. Concert hall quality.

Paul shakes his head, but thankfully doesn't ask more. Instead he turns to Brian. "You got somewhere Duncan can set up while we have our meeting? And then after we'll have a chat about resourcing."

Brian shrugs. "In here should be right. It's just me and Dom in the office today, and he won't bug ya none."

A few minutes later I'm settled at the table with my laptop and a cup of coffee while Paul and Brian head off to his office, and all I can think is that we have a four-hour drive back to Perth later, and I'm pretty sure Paul is going to have questions. Not about resourcing, either.

I'm actually pretty revved when we get back in the car for the long drive back to Perth. I powered through my emails, checked in with my team before they went home, got Dom to introduce me to a few people hanging around the site, and then Paul, Brian, and I had a quick look through the resourcing plan and decided where to move guys around to and where to put the New Zealanders. Technically, it's not Brian's job to worry about anything but his own site, but when a bloke has forty years' experience, you'd be an idiot not to take advantage of it. There's a reason Paul brought Brian down from the northern part of the state to work on this site—he's smart, he's experienced, and he gets shit done. Kind of like Paul himself. If Brian had wanted to make the move to project manager, he could have. I asked him a couple years back why he hadn't, and he'd laughed hard enough that I worried he'd piss himself, and then asked me if I really thought he was cut out for the politics of it.

Er. No.

Needless to say, the atmosphere in the car as we begin the drive is vastly different from this morning. Paul is relaxed—well, as relaxed as a PM who's under the pump can be—and rather than him sending out vibes like he wants to murder me and bury my body beside the highway, we're actually *chatting*. Mostly project talk, but still—what more can I expect from a colleague?

Don't answer that, Dunc.

"So, you've been out to sites before?" he asks, and his curiosity is clear. Can't blame him—like I said, it's not really part of my job description.

I shrug. "Sometimes that's the easiest way to find out what's needed," I admit, and then add bluntly, "A lot of the time, site guys don't want to take calls from anyone in head office. They consider us all wankers who have no idea what really happens on a site." He winces but doesn't argue. "They're not wrong, most of the time, but that doesn't mean we can't help. The company pays us to help. We just need someone on site to tell us what they need."

He sighs. "Yeah. I wish I could tell you I've always valued and respected the input of your people"—I laugh so hard that I snort, and he throws a wry grin my way—"but when I was working sites back in the day, I considered everyone from head office to be a wanker in a suit."

"Not much has changed," I jibe, and it's his turn to laugh.

"Mostly it has," he concedes, "since a lot of the time I'm the wanker from the city office now, even if I do avoid suits as much as possible. But then I'll run into someone like your predecessor, and all my old prejudices rise up."

"Mate, I never met the man, never spoke to him, but from everything I've heard, you weren't the one in the wrong. I just wish he hadn't screwed the pooch for the rest of us."

"You're doing a good job of fixing things," he says quietly, and warmth spreads through my chest.

"Thanks. Uh, so yeah, I try to get out to sites occasionally, especially the rural ones. Metro sites are easy, you know? The guys rotate in and out of the office all the time, and most of them know who I am by sight if nothing else and can always find a way to bitch me out if something's not right. I once had a guy trap me at the urinal and not let me leave until he'd finished whining about needing an extra set of hands on his team. But the rural guys don't get that opportunity. Plus, since they think of me as a city wanker, they wouldn't take it if they had it. So...." I shrug.

"Usually once I get the chance to talk to them in person, they work out that I'm not that bad."

"I wouldn't go that far," he teases. Yes, Paul Hanks is *teasing me.*

No lie, my heart beats a tiny bit faster. Is this just collegiate teasing?

Or...?

I force a laugh and tell myself not to be stupid. The conversation turns to some of the rural sites he's worked on and I've visited, and from there I learn that Paul, too, is a country boy, although he grew up on a dairy farm in Victoria as opposed to my station in the Pilbara.

Before I know it, twilight falls, then night, and the twinkling lights of Greater Perth surround us. We drive through the suburbs, and it occurs to me that I don't know where Paul lives. I mean, are we driving past his place right now? Does dropping me off in the city mean that he'll have to double back?

"You can just dump me here," I blurt, cutting him off midsentence. Because apparently that's the kind of thing I do now.

He shoots me a glance. "What?"

I huff a small laugh. "I mean, is it out of your way to take me back into the city? You can drop me off somewhere if it is, and I'll get the train or an Uber or something."

"Oh. No, it's not out of my way. Well... not really." He hesitates while I wonder what he means by that. "Are you hungry? We could get something to eat."

"Yes!" *Too eager, Dunc.* "I mean, yeah, I could definitely eat." That's better. Casual. He's probably just hungry. He's probably just planning to feed the out-of-town colleague. After all, it's a great way to eat out and bill it to the project.

I look out the side window and wince. That's probably

not it. I like to think my company is more appealing than just a free meal.

"Do you have any preferences? Perth's not quite Melbourne for foodie culture, but there are a lot of great places."

I laugh, because when it comes to food, I'm the least picky person on the planet. "Mate, I ate fried cockroaches in China. I'll try anything once, and probably eat it again later too."

That gets us started on all the different foods we've eaten while traveling, and it seems like only moments later that we're cruising through the CBD.

"Where are you staying?" Paul asks. I tell him—it's right down the street from the office—and he makes a left turn. "There's a pretty decent Thai place in the hotel," he says. "We order from there when we're working late."

"Sounds good," I say, and it does, but that's not why my mouth is suddenly watering. Oh no. That's entirely because Paul is going to be in a hotel with me.

Granted, it'll be in a restaurant, but my stupid, suddenly-teenage-again hormones don't care about that.

He parks the car in the same lot we got it from this morning, and I grab my laptop bag. It's just a block to the hotel, but the streets are pretty much deserted—this area is mostly office buildings. It lends a weird feeling of intimacy to the walk, like we're the only two people in the city. Like nothing is real. Like if I reached out and grabbed Paul's hand, it would be okay, because we're in a bubble that's insulated from reality, and in that bubble I know Paul would welcome the touch.

Then we get close to the hotel and there are people coming out, noise, light, and the bubble bursts. Maybe Paul *would* welcome a come-on from me, but given how volatile the situation was between us only this morning, I can't risk it. There's a lot on the line for me right now, for him, and for the project. We need to be able to work together, and that means me not putting us in potentially awkward positions.

There's no rush, anyway. Now that we're on speaking terms, I can build a friendship between us, be a bit flirty, let things develop over time. It doesn't all have to be tonight.

Lost in my thoughts, I hang back a bit. My gaze drops to Paul's arse.

I wish it was tonight.

six

NOVEMBER

I NEVER HAD a pen pal when I was a kid. Never got to know someone via correspondence. Every friendship I've ever had has been built face-to-face. Until now. Sometimes I go through my phone and randomly read the texts Paul and I send each other and marvel at the fact that I'm just as comfortable talking to him as I am with friends I've had for years.

PAUL

Found this great Nepalese place today, reminded me of what you said about dried yak cheese.

DUNCAN

Did you get any?

PAUL

Nah, they didn't have it. The dal bhat rocked, though.

DUNCAN

Damn it, now I want Nepalese.

DUNCAN

Okay, I gave in and watched the 1st episode of Game of Thrones—and then the next 3 after that. You were right, I'm hooked. Can't believe I thought it wouldn't be my thing.

PAUL

Right? I never liked fantasy, but that show is fuckin' awesome.

DUNCAN

I'm trying to decide if I want to get online and find out what happens or avoid spoilers.

PAUL

You don't need to go online. I can give you everything you want.

PAUL

You still up?

DUNCAN

Mate, it's three hours later here.

PAUL

So… yes?

DUNCAN

Well, I am now. What's up?

PAUL

Nothing. Back from Friday night drinks at the pub and thought I'd say hello. What's on for the weekend?

DUNCAN

Tomorrow I'll be sleeping in to make up for being woken. Are you going to want to text all night?

INCOMING CALL FROM PAUL HANKS

DUNCAN

Are you watching the draft?

PAUL

You're joking, right? Too fucking boring.

DUNCAN

LIE!

PAUL

Okay, maybe it's on in the background while I do the requisitions.

DUNCAN

So you saw my Eagles steal young Jones from under the Tigers' nose? LOL

PAUL

Don't be a dick, Dunc. Or at least try not to. I know that's hard for you.

DUNCAN

I feel like I should be making an innuendo about dicks being hard.

PAUL

Maybe you should.

seven

DECEMBER 3

MY PHONE VIBRATES in front of me on the table in the meeting room, and I spare it a quick glance as I wrap up the meeting with my team. It's a text from Paul, and I resolutely pull my gaze away. If it was urgent, he'd call, which means it's either not time sensitive or not work related.

Yeah, that's right. Paul and I text about personal stuff. A lot. *A lot*, a lot. Like, this is his third text to me today, and it's not even lunchtime. We're kind of dating.

Except not really.

Well... not at all.

I think.

It's confusing.

At first I thought it was just confusing for me, but then last week I ran it past some friends over drinks, and they were all confused too.

Let me see if I can run it down for you.

That first night, Paul and I lingered over dinner, talking until the restaurant closed. He insisted on paying, then did so with cash and didn't take the receipt. That means he

159

can't claim the cost back against the project, which means he bought me dinner out of his own pocket, even though he could have claimed it. So... kind of a date, right? Especially since we didn't talk about work at all.

But then we parted ways at the restaurant door with a mere "See you later." No lingering looks. Definitely no kiss. Not even a handshake. Not date-like at all.

I stayed in Perth for the following two days, working with Paul and Rachel to get the contractors sorted out and make sure things were ready for the New Zealanders to arrive. It was also a great excuse to spend time with Paul and get to know him better. During those two days, we had lunch and dinner together twice—in fact, I delayed my flight home on the Friday night so I could join the team at the pub for Friday night drinks and then have dinner with Paul. Now, that's kind of date-ish, right? Or is it just my colleague keeping me company while I'm in a strange city? Although, he knows I went to boarding school and uni in Perth and it's in no way a strange city to me.

Confused yet? Just wait, there's more.

The Monday after I left Perth, I got a completely unnecessary text from Paul to tell me that the New Zealand team had arrived and was being inducted and transferred out to site and thanking me for getting them on board. I texted back to say he was welcome. Somehow (and even though I've read over the text string a dozen times, I still *am not sure how*), we went from talking about work to a conversation about what we did on the weekend, and from there to what we were doing the following weekend.

Since then, we've texted every day. We talk on the phone at least twice a week, although admittedly that's sometimes for work. We've definitely crossed the line from colleagues to friends, but I'm not sure yet if we've also crossed the line to something more. Some of our conversations are slightly flirty, but not overtly so. Sometimes I think he's definitely interested, that we're basically long-distance dating and if we were in the same city we'd be fucking by now, but then other times I wonder if we're just friends and my wishful thinking is reading too much into it.

I guess what it comes down to is that I have to make a definite move. It was always the plan; I just hoped that I'd be more sure of what his response would be.

"So, in the grand tradition of this team," I conclude, grinning at my people, "we've totally kicked arse and are on top of things. Great work, everyone." It's true. Jimmy lit a bonfire under the PMs and rollout teams in the eastern states, and together with an intensive resourcing push, it got things moving. We're now only four days behind schedule, and if we can keep up the pace and nothing goes wrong, that time should be made up by the time embargo rolls around. We're all afraid to say it out loud in case we jinx ourselves, but it looks like we may just make the deadline for stage one.

We're still massively overbudget, of course—more so now, in fact, since an intensive resourcing push costs money—but Paul and I have managed to stem the arterial bleed in the WASANT resourcing budget and put together a comprehensive plan showing that resourcing for stage two won't need anywhere near that much money. He, Jimmy, and I are confident that if we meet the deadline, the board won't even mention the budget except in passing.

The meeting breaks up, and as everyone gathers their stuff and makes their way out, I pick up my phone, a delicious lick of anticipation sending butterflies through my system.

PAUL:

> In the interest of saving project money—

Oh. It's a work message. Well, that's okay. Maybe it'll be a good excuse to call him.

> —I think I should stay with you when I'm in Melbourne for the stage one wrapup.

What. The. Fuck.

WHAT THE FUCK!

What does that *mean*?

I slump into my chair at the conference table and stare at my phone. You'd think that having the guy I've been sort-of flirting with invite himself to stay with me would be a positive thing, but I'm just as confused as ever.

The way I see it, there are three possible meanings to this message. The first is that he's incredibly conscious of how tight the project budget is (and how far over it we've run) and is genuinely thinking to save money by not staying in a hotel. If I say no, he'll probably just ask someone else here who he knows well.

The second is that we're friends, hotels are boring, and he figures the trip will be more fun if he invites himself to stay with me. Which is all true, and most likely the actual meaning.

The third....

I take a deep, shaky breath. The third possible meaning is that he's making a move.

So which is it? Because there's a big difference between meaning one and meaning three. It all comes down to whether "in the interest of saving project money" was said seriously or not. With anyone else, I'd say no emoji means that it's serious, not tongue-in-cheek, but

Paul never uses emojis. We've talked about that before—rather sternly on my part. I believe I may have told him that a failure to embrace the emoji is indicative of sociopathy. He laughed—a lot—and then told me that anyone over the age of forty who loves emojis as much as I do is going through a serious midlife crisis. I hung up on him and then texted a string of emojis that told him what I thought of that.

So yeah. No emojis from Paul. Which means he could very well be sending a flirty come-on, but it reads like a business proposition to a colleague.

In desperation, I screenshot the text, open a group chat with my friends, and ask their opinion, explaining the whole no-emojis thing.

What follows is a flurry of WTFs, lewd suggestions, and demands for a picture so they can assess his worthiness before offering advice. I'm just about to swear at them and close the app when Ethan, who is probably the most sensible of us, sends a response.

> Do you really need to know now? Say "sure" and work out the details later. If he's making a move, you'll probably be able to tell when he arrives and STAYS WITH YOU.

Huh.

I mean, it doesn't satisfy my burning need to know how Paul feels about me, but Ethan's right. The stage one wrap-up isn't for a week and a half, so even if Paul thinks it's meaning one or two, I have time to continue my sneaky wooing (wooage? Or maybe I should go with another word altogether. Seduction?) and by the time he gets here, it may have changed to meaning three. I can make up the bed in the spare-slash-storage room *and* make sure I'm stocked up on condoms and lube. Which gets used can be a last-minute revelation.

Thanks, E.

I switch back to Paul's text thread.

DUNCAN:

Sounds like a plan ;-)

DECEMBER 12

Nervous? Me? No. I'm not nervous.

"Dunc, are you okay?"

I jump, sloshing coffee over the side of my mug. Thankfully it's not too hot. I busy myself cleaning up the small spill and ignore Jimmy's question. I really have no excuse for my behaviour this morning. If I tell people the truth, they're going to think it's weird.

Paul is coming.

After over a month of texts and phone calls and becoming friends (and maybe more) but never seeing each other in person, he's going to be here. In the same room as me. *Staying at my place.*

Yesterday, I overheard Jimmy asking one the of project admins if the travel plans for the incoming PMs were all in place, and she told him she still didn't have Paul Hanks's hotel reservation. So Jimmy rang him right then to make sure he'd have a place to stay, then hung up and told the admin Paul was staying with a friend.

Which of course raised a whole heap of questions in my

busy little brain. Yes—Paul considers me a friend. Is it more than that, though? If it was just friendship or colleague-ship, wouldn't he have just said to Jimmy, "I'm staying with Duncan"?

Am I overthinking this?

Yes. Yes, I am.

Hence my ridiculous distraction this morning. And the nerves.

The meeting this morning—well, it'll actually take most of the day—is to go over every part of stage one prior to official completion and go-live tomorrow. That's right, bitches, *completion and go-live*. We've made it. We've done it. Embargo begins in two days, and stage one is all but complete.

We're not celebrating yet, not until the rollout is live. Everything should be perfect, but until it actually happens, you never know, right?

So the senior project team is gathering today for a final checklist. Most of it will be ridiculously technical and won't require me, but Jimmy requested I attend to provide a fresh set of eyes and ears and show solidarity.

I agreed, because it means I get to spend the whole day in the same room as Paul. And isn't that just sad? I'm actu-ally ashamed of myself for being so sappy.

Paul's flight was delayed, so we're basically waiting for him. Between the time difference and flight duration, it's a bitch coming from Perth to Melbourne for a morning meet-ing. In fact, the only way to do it is to get an 11:30 p.m. flight for a 5:00 a.m. arrival, or else leave Perth in the late after-noon and stay over the night before the meeting. Paul had to make sure everything was wrapped up before he left, so he opted for the midnight flight... and ended up waiting at the airport until three in the morning for it to depart. His plane landed a little over an hour ago, and he's been stuck in a cab on the Tulla trying to get into the city since. And every minute I've been waiting feels like an eternity.

There's a small commotion outside the room, and then the door opens and Paul walks in.

"Sorry I'm late, fucking Qantas couldn't find a screwdriver or some shit," he announces, dumping a small overnight bag beside the door and bringing his laptop bag over to the table. There's an empty seat beside me, and even though it means walking past two other empty chairs, he manages to make choosing it the most natural thing in the world. And then he's sitting next to me, the big bulk of him folding into the chair, radiating warmth. I can smell him, and that's what makes it hit home that he's actually, finally here. His delicious smell.

He flashes me a smile, and *hello*, getting hard.

"You made it, so we're good," Jimmy says, and all attention turns to him as he opens the meeting.

It's going to be a long day.

I drop my keys twice before I manage to get my front door open. Paul laughs about it, and I want to be embarrassed, but how can I be when I've made him laugh?

It's going to be so bad for me if he just wants to be friends.

"Just dump your bag there for now," I tell him, tossing the keys on the console next to the door that I bought just for that purpose and dropping my laptop bag too. "I'll give you the twenty-cent tour."

He's still grinning as he closes the door and drops his bags next to mine.

"Living area and kitchen." I wave at the open-plan space, which is actually a pretty great size for an apartment in South Yarra, and then head toward the short hallway. "Bathroom is here"—I open the door on my way past so he can see it—"and this is the spare room-slash-office-slash storage room." I hesitate, then push open my bedroom door. "And this is my room."

He peers into the spare room, then saunters past me into *my bedroom*. Paul Hanks is in my bedroom, and his big, warm body brushed against mine when he entered. My mouth is so fucking dry right now.

He walks over to stand beside the bed and looks around. It's nothing special, really—bed, nightstands, dresser, wardrobe, rug. The view from the window isn't bad, but it's not exactly a selling point either. At least I made the bed this morning.

Turning to face me, he raises an eyebrow. "Are you just going to stand there?"

For a long moment, I don't understand. Then he raises his hand to his shirt and begins unbuttoning it, and awareness comes crashing in on me.

"Oh thank fuck!"

I'm by his side without realising I've moved, brushing his hands away so I can strip him myself. He grabs my face instead, his grip firm but not rough, and tips my head back. I'm about to complain that I can't see what I'm doing when his face descends and his lips are on mine.

I instantly forget about his shirt. About breathing. About anything but his warm, soft mouth, the taste of him, the feel of his hard, huge body against me, the way every nerve ending in my body seems to be firing from the wild, crazy pleasure of his touch.

He lifts his head, and we're both breathing hard. His pupils are blown, his lips wet. His gaze searches my face.

"Okay?" he asks, and I laugh, a crazy, demented sound, and reach up to yank his mouth back down to mine.

It's hours before we lie in the quiet darkness of my bedroom, finally spent. A lot of people think engineers are stodgy, but let me tell you, creativity and out-of-the-box thinking are strengths every good engineer has, and Paul has more than proved that he's a good engineer.

I'm listening to his breathing, my hand twined with his just because I can, when he stirs and says, "Is there any chance you can work out of the Perth office for a while?"

My heart beats faster. "Yeah." I keep my voice level. "It should be okay. I might have to go back and forth some-times." It really shouldn't be a problem—we work for a telco, remember? I can handle almost everything via phone or video conference.

"I'd come here, but—"

"You're the PM for WASANT, Paul," I say, unable to keep from sounding exasperated. "You need to be living in one of the states you're overseeing." I hesitate. "I actually thought we'd be doing long-distance." In the moments I allowed myself to fantasize that he wanted more than just friend-ship, that is. I thought we'd have to work up to being in the same city.

His hand tenses slightly. "Is that what you want to do?"

I laugh and roll over on top of him and kiss his startled mouth. "No, you dipshit. I've been going out of my mind wanting you here, or wanting to be there, or just wanting to be with you." I pause. "I've also been going out of my mind wondering if you want the same. You're fucking hard to read, mate."

He frowns. "Whaddaya mean? We've pretty much been together since you came to Perth. I mean, maybe we haven't been on any actual dates since that first one, but we talk every day. Some of my site guys don't talk to their wives that often."

I just kiss him again. There's plenty of time for us to argue about this; right now, I have other things on my mind.

DECEMBER 13

THERE'S a low-level murmur of excitement in the office. Very few people are actually working; instead, we're all gathered near the Titan project team's desks. There's champagne chilling in tubs, beer, food waiting to be served, but none of it will be touched until the go-live is successful.

And if it's not... well, we'll still be drinking, but it won't be a party.

It should be fine, though. Yesterday's meeting covered off every tiny detail. The design engineers are all brilliant, and they've been over everything a million times. The rollout hasn't been a picnic, but there's no reason to think anything isn't right.

Still, most of the senior project team looks nervous. Me included.

I glance over at Paul, standing five feet away talking to Dean Grech. We talked about it last night and decided to wait until after the go-live to spring our relationship on our colleagues. Everyone's kind of distracted now. We'll talk to Jimmy first, on Monday, and then to our respective line managers, and with the way the company gossip mill works, everyone will know before the end of the day, but for tonight, we're being discreet.

I'm really rethinking that decision right now. I could desperately use a hand to cling to.

"Okay, here we go," the design team leader announces. He gets up from the laptop he's been working at and offers the chair to Jimmy. "It's all ready for you."

The office falls silent as Jimmy takes a seat. I feel someone come up beside me and glance over to see Krista.

"Exciting," she murmurs. "Aren't you glad you're here for this?"

She's talking about the incredible high of working on a project that's changing telecommunications in our country, but I can't stop myself from stealing another look at Paul.

"Yeah."

At the laptop, Jimmy hits a key, then types something. He's entering a password. He pauses. Takes a deep breath. Then hits another key.

We all wait in dead silence. If it worked, if the design is sound and the rollout was done properly, the network should be going live. The engineers monitoring it should start calling status reports any—

There's a jumble of shouts, site names being called out, and the office explodes into cheers. I grab Krista in a tight hug as she shrieks victoriously, then let her go and go to congratulate my team and everyone else.

By the time I get to Jimmy, he's got some colour back in his face and a bottle of beer in his hand. He and the state project managers are huddled around the laptop, checking to see which sites failed, but they don't look upset, so there can't be too many. Paul is outright grinning, and I figure WASANT is in pretty good shape.

"Duncan!" Jimmy grabs me in a hug. "We did it, mate. Couldn't have done it without you."

"I second that," Paul says, and I smile and murmur something self-deprecating. I mean, they're right, but big-noting myself isn't going to look good. It's all about the *team*, right?

The wicked glance Paul shoots me gives me the feeling he knows what I'm thinking.

"Jimmy, phone! It's the client," someone calls, and Jimmy laughs raucously.

"Fuck yeah, it's the client! No penalties for them!" He puts down his beer. "We kicked stage one arse. Bring on stage two!"

As Jimmy goes to take the client's call, presumably with a little more professional decorum, Paul comes to stand next to me. In the press of the crowd, nobody will notice if we're standing a little too close, if our hands touch. And it doesn't really matter if they do, because after Monday, we'll be publicly a couple. I'll be working out of the Perth office and mostly living at Paul's place. And we're going to kick this project's arse.

Bring on stage two.

swept under

A SHORT SUMMER INTERLUDE

swept under

What better way to spend a hot summer day than at the beach with friends? Diving into the waves is the perfect way for Alex to cool off... until he gets tangled up with sexy surfer Dylan—literally.

Dylan seems fine with it, though... more than fine. Suddenly Alex's day at the beach has turned into the perfect hot summer interlude.

one hot summer day...

I SURFACE INTO THE HOT, bright day and swipe the salt water from my face, ready to go again. There's nothing quite so invigorating on a stifling summer day as diving into the cool, refreshing waves that pound the local beach.

Well, except sex. But I haven't gotten any of that lately, so jumping into waves will just have to do.

While I wait for the next dive-worthy wave, I glance over at my friends, lined up in the almost waist-deep water. It's been ages since we've all been able to get together like this for a casual day of beach fun. I smile, and it must be sappier than usual, because Dave, who's standing beside me, gives me a weird look.

"What?" he asks.

"Nothing." I shake my head and look back out to the water. If I tell him I've missed him, I'll never hear the end of it. Especially since it's partly my fault—I've been really caught up in work lately and skipped a few nights out.

Pushing aside thoughts of work, I let my attention snag

on a surfer a little way out. I've always had a soft spot for surfers—after all, that's how I first realized I was gay. Sitting on the beach every day before school, watching the surfers master the waves… staring avidly at the guys coming out of the water and unzipping their wetsuits. It took me a while to catch on that I was more interested in that last part than anything they did on the water. I got to be very good at guessing which ones would give me the best show once they reached the sand, though. I'm a little rusty now, but this one looks like he'd be prime material for my spank bank. I wonder if—

"Alex!" Dave snaps, and I jerk my attention to the wave bearing down on us. *Fuck!* Belatedly, I dive into it, but I'm just a fraction too late, and it sweeps me under.

We're so close to dry sand that I know I just have to hold on a few moments, but it's hard not to panic when water's filling your nose and tumbling you ass-over-teakettle. Something catches against my leg—seaweed, maybe?—and then a body thunks against my side. *Dave!* I grab on tight, grateful to have this contact with the world beyond the wave, determined not to get lost again in the maelstrom of the ocean.

Yeah, yeah, I'm the dramatic type.

Sure enough, a few seconds that feel like hours later, the wave deposits me on the wet sand in the shallows and sweeps back out to sea. I keep my eyes closed against the sun and turn my head to the side to hack up what feels like liters of seawater that seem to have taken up residence in my lungs. I'm so busy coughing and spluttering that I completely forget to let go of Dave… until I hear his voice.

"Alex, what the fuck, mate? I didn't know you were that hard up."

I wheeze for air. "Ha fucking ha," I mumble, then realize his voice came from above me.

Oh no.

I slit my eyes open against the brightness, just enough to make out my smirking friends standing in a semicircle around me. All my friends.

Oh no.

I let go of whoever it is I've been clutching for dear life and scramble into a sitting position. The water ebbs and flows gently around my legs, but I'm too worried about dying of humiliation to enjoy it. Screwing up my courage, I peer down at the stranger still lying in the shallows beside me.

He smirks back. "Hi."

Fuck. Did he have to be sexy, with his longish wet hair all tousled around his face and his raspy voice and warm brown eyes and a fucking dimple, for fuck's sake? Who has a sexy dimple outside of TV? Is it even allowed?

"I'm so, so, so, *so* very sorry," I manage, taking in more details about him, like his long, rangy body outlined by his rashie... and the surfboard attached to his ankle that's washed up on his other side. "You just had to be a surfer, didn't you?" I accuse, then slap my hand over my mouth as my friends—who all know about how surfers triggered my sexual awakening—laugh so hard, I think Dave might actually die. Or maybe that's wishful thinking.

I want to apologize again to the sexy surfer, but I'm scared of what might come out if I take my hand away. He's still smiling, albeit somewhat quizzically now, and he gracefully rises to a sitting position *without using his hands.* Seriously. Mine fall to my sides in shock. The guy must have abs of steel, and right at this second, I can't think of anything I want more than to stroke them.

"Really?" he says, and I blink. Behind me, one of my ex-friends makes a choking noise.

"Really what?"

His smile turns into what can only be called a leer as he slowly peels off his rashie. Helpless to resist, my gaze follows, my breathing speeding up as each glorious inch is revealed... tanned skin... a trail of hair leading up... and who knew a belly button could be so erotic? The ripple of washboard abs—

Wait.

Abs.

Oh *fucking fuck me!*

I tear my gaze from his altogether too tempting stomach and chest as he pulls the rashie over his head and look back at his face. "I said it out loud, didn't I?"

He nods.

"I am *so* sorry. Well... mostly," honesty makes me add as I sneak another peek at his torso.

"No worries," he says, casually stretching his arms up over his head in a way that makes everything ripple beautifully and my jaw drop in admiration. "It's always nice to have people notice the hard work." He extends his hand to me. "I'm Dylan."

I shake it automatically, hoping I'm not drooling. "Alex."

"Nice to meet you, Alex."

Before I can think of a reply that doesn't sound creepy —*the pleasure's allllll mine*—he springs to his feet in one lithe movement, then pulls me up with him. Of course, I don't look all graceful like he does—and I certainly don't manage to do it hands-free. Even with his help, I still end up clambering upright. It's not entirely due to me being a klutz, though. We're in three inches of flowing water and the sand isn't a stable surface. That's my story, and I'm sticking to it.

"So, Alex," he begins as I shake my hand to get the sticky wet sand off it and somehow end up splattering him with it. He pretends not to notice, and I swear, my infatuation grows.

"Sorry," I mumble again, then realize my not-sandy hand is still holding his. I yank it back, almost overbalancing, but am rescued from falling on my ass by him grabbing my arms and hauling me closer to him.

I'm not usually this much of a bumbling idiot. Sure, nobody's ever called me smooth, but most of the time I can remain on my own two feet and control what comes out of my mouth.

But then, most of the time I haven't been washed ashore clutching a walking wet dream of a man.

Once he's sure I'm steady, he lets go of one arm, but slides his hand down the other—making me shiver despite the hot sun—and takes my hand.

"That's better," he murmurs, smiling at me, and it seems I'm in luck. My brain seems to have shut down in sheer embarrassment, because I don't say or do anything weird. Instead, I smile back.

"I hope I didn't knock you off your board or anything," I manage. I'm pretty sure I would have felt an impact like that, but who knows.

"Nah." He rubs his thumb back and forth over the back of my hand, and my waterlogged dick comes out of its coma, twitching. *No. No! Do* not *get hard now.* The last thing I need is to be kicked off the beach for lewd behavior or something while the man of my dreams watches.

Although, if we were on a private beach, I wouldn't mind having the aforementioned man of my dreams watch me engage in lewd behavior.

Shaking my head to dispel that thought, I say, "Thanks for letting me use you as a touchstone. It was nice to have someone to hold on to while I wondered if I'd ever breathe again."

He laughs, a warm, rich sound that has a lot of other beachgoers turning around.

"I'm happy to be your touchstone anytime," he assures me. "Are you okay now? Let me buy you a Coke or something while you get your feet back under you."

Aw, that's sweet.

"Thanks, but you don't need to d— Ow!"

I lift my free hand to rub the back of my head and glare over my shoulder at Dave.

"Whoops! Did I accidentally smack you? So sorry! Here, let me look!" Dave grabs my head in both hands and leans in, hissing, "Say yes, moron! He's flirting!"

He's... what?

Oh my *god*!

Dave leans back and lets go as he sees awareness dawn on me. "Looks okay to me. Just a tap. Sorry, mate! Listen, why don't you sit this one out? You look kinda pale. I'm sure Dylan here will keep you company till we get back."

"Sure," Dylan agrees immediately, squeezing my hand. "I'd love to."

Say something.

Words. Now!

"Great!" I blurt.

Dave snorts and joins the rest of my chortling friends while I just stand there in the shallows, my feet sinking into the waterlogged sand as I hold hands with a guy I've known for a whole five minutes and yet have already spooned.

"C'mon." Dylan lets go of me long enough to scoop up his board, then tugs me out of the water and onto the hard-packed sand. "Let me dump this rashie and my board at the car, then we'll find a Mr. Whippy."

I don't know what makes me say it. I really, really don't. I'm an Aussie. I grew up with Mr. Whippy ice-cream trucks. I know exactly what he's talking about and why. And when it comes to sex, I'm the most vanilla person you will *ever* meet.

"Ooh, I like a kinky man."

But for some reason, I say it anyway.

He gives me a startled glance, then bursts out laughing.

Fuck infatuation. I think I'm in love.

Despite my protests that I should be treating him, Dylan insists on buying me an ice cream and a Coke. We sit in the warm dry sand to enjoy them, letting the sun dry our hair as we stare out at the sparkling blue water and chat. Well, he might be staring at the water. I'm staring at him. And it seems like he's looking back at me a lot of the time, so maybe there's not so much staring at the water. But we're definitely chatting.

"So when the talking heads on TV are spouting about 'economists say,' it's you they're referring to?" I ask. I've never actually met an economist in real life. I didn't think it was a job ordinary people had.

He chuckles. "Not me specifically... well, not always. The study I'm working on is specifically about how climate change affects the economy and what economic strategies we can use to become carbon neutral. Our team does get quoted a lot in news reports about climate change and environment." It's hard to tell if his cheeks are pink because of the sun or if he's blushing, but the bashful smile makes me think it's the latter.

"That's so awesome," I enthuse. "I like that a lot better than if you were just helping rich people get richer." I pat his arm, then end up leaving my hand there because it feels nice.

His gaze meets mine, brown eyes warm. "I like it too," he says softly, and like magnets drawn together, we lean in. His lips brush mine lightly, just a graze, then return for a short kiss, then again, again, and then I throw decorum to the wind and yank him close.

He tastes like seawater and Coke and soft-serve ice cream, which is a weird combination but also the best thing I ever tasted. His lips are slightly chapped, but so soft, and I would gladly sit right here in the sand kissing him until—

"Get a room!"

I pull back amidst the sound of laughter and heckling and flip off the group of teenage boys who clearly have nothing better to do.

"Er," I begin, feeling like I should apologize but not sure why. It's not my fault a group of fifteen-year-olds think they're funny.

"If there was anywhere private around here, I'd be dragging you there right now," Dylan whispers. It takes a second for his words to sink in, and then I whip my head around, desperately searching for anything—*anything*—that could provide a degree of privacy. The public toilets are my first thought, but there's a steady stream of people coming and going from there. I might have risked it anyway, but a lot of them are kids, and jail is not on my to-do list. Dylan's car? But no... the parking lot is also crowded with beachgoers arriving and departing. Surely there has to be a semiprivate hedge somewhere?

Dylan chuckles. "Relax. We'll get our chance. What are you doing tonight?"

I nod frantically. "Great idea! Tonight. Your place? We can use mine, but Dave's my roommate." I squint, wondering if there's any way I can convince him to go out without letting him know Dylan's coming over.

His warm, calloused hand cups my cheek, and my gaze instantly lifts to clash with his. "My place is fine, but how about dinner first?"

For long seconds, I just blink at him. Dinner? Is he... asking me on a date?

"You want to go on a date with me?"

He grins, flashing beautiful white teeth. "Yes."

"Why?" Instantly, I pull back from his hand, slapping mine over my eyes. "Oh my god, I did *not* just ask that." I wish a huge wave would come and sweep me away from this humiliation.

His laugh wraps around me like a hug, and I peek between two fingers. He's looking at me fondly, like I'm special and amusing, and I slowly lower my hand.

"What I meant to say was... that sounds great."

I've been wined and dined and romanced... and now I'm doing my best to get fucked. I don't think it's going to be hard—or rather, it *is*, heh heh heh. Very hard. And throbbing. There's something incredibly arousing about Dylan being so turned on because of me.

We're lying on his couch, mostly naked, our clothes

strewn in a trail from the front door. He didn't bother to turn on the lights when we arrived—we were both too busy trying to find each other's tonsils with our tongues—so the only illumination is from ambient light through the window as we writhe together in the dimness, enjoying the full-body contact and the long, drugging kisses. Anyone who tells you kissing is a waste of time is delusional—I could spend months just kissing Dylan.

Not right now, though.

Right now, my focus is the steel rod in my hand.

"Tighter," Dylan gasps, thrusting into my grip as he breaks our kiss, and I oblige. His moan is the highest praise.

"Lube?" I ask, licking the corded line of his throat. How can he possibly taste this good? It's just skin.

"Uhhhhhhh..." His eyes roll back as I stroke, and I abandon any hope of getting a sensible answer. Where are my pants?

I prop myself on an elbow and squint into the darkness. There! I knew I'd been close to the couch when I finally got them off. I reach out, but they're just beyond my fingertips.

"Alex," Dylan begs, twining his leg through mine and trailing his hand down my spine. I shudder, the sensation going right through me, and stretch. So... close...

I fall off the couch.

"Alex?" Sounding much more alert, Dylan sits up and peers down at me. "You okay?"

Snatching up my pants, I wave them triumphantly. "Lube!" I grab the packet from my pocket, where I stashed it while telling myself it was "just in case" but totally hoping to use it.

He laughs and grabs my arm. "Get back up here. I don't know if I can wait long enough to prep."

"Frottage?" I suggest, scrambling back onto the couch. We were already doing that anyway. "Or I could blow you?"

He lies back on the couch, knees bent and feet planted, and opens his legs, giving me one hell of a view, even in the dark. "Fuck my taint," he says, and I don't need to be asked twice. In seconds, I'm lubed up and squeezing his thighs closed around my dick.

The visceral sound he makes as I begin to thrust goes straight to my cock and drives me to move faster. He tightens his muscles, and the hot, wet tunnel becomes cock heaven. I brace myself, changing angle slightly, and the next thrust makes him cry out as I rub against his most sensitive bits, at the same time catching his dick between our bodies.

He squeezes again, and we both cry out this time. I let my forehead drop to his shoulder for one last thrust...

When I can think again, I'm collapsed on top of Dylan, face pressed against his throat, cradled between his sprawled legs. His chest is heaving as he pants, and for a second I worry that I'm crushing him, but when I try to move, his arms constrict around me.

"That," he gasps, "was fucking amazing."

I nuzzle against the side of his face. "Phenomenal." We're both sweaty and sticky, and cum is going cold and gross on our skin, but I can't bring myself to care. Maybe when I have the energy to move, I can talk him into a shared shower.

Our breathing starts to settle, and we lie twined together, gradually relaxing.

"Got plans for the rest of the weekend?" he asks at last, stroking a hand down my arm.

I smile into the dark. "Not really. You?"

"Wanna come surfing with me tomorrow morning?"

I laugh. "Mate, did you not see me today? Surfing is a bit beyond my coordination level." I pause, then add, "But I'll sit on the beach and perv on you while you surf. And I'll buy you breakfast after."

"Done," he says promptly. "Sex, surfing, and food. The perfect weekend."

He's not wrong about that.

diving in deep

diving in deep

Cameron is sick of being a stereotypical nerd. In an attempt to "reinvent" himself, he takes three months off for a holiday in Australia—something the old Cameron would never do.

Troy and Jake are in a committed relationship. Co-owners of Sail Away, a water sport and cruising company, their life is about sun, sea, and each other.

Neither Troy nor Jake have ever participated in a ménage, but after a day on the water with Cameron, both are fantasizing about sandwiching him between them. Cameron has never been with a man but can't stop thinking about the hot couple, and how they'd look, naked and entwined. When he walks in on them having sex in the underwater observatory, he can't look away—and then they invite him to join in.

Will the old Cameron sink in uncharted territory? Or will the new Cameron find himself diving in deep?

prologue

THE PLANE BANKED, and Cameron Hall stared out the window. Sunlight glittered off the ocean below. As the plane leveled again, he turned his head and gazed out the window across the aisle. Lush green rainforest covered hills and valleys.

He'd never seen so much nature in his life. What the hell was he doing here?

Relax. The old Cameron, the geeky data management expert, might be uncomfortable outside cities with a minimum population of two million, but he wasn't that person anymore. Didn't want to be that person, the guy everyone smirked at and pitied. The stereotype. The new Cameron, who did crazy things like take three months off work to go to far-north Australia, he would be fine. The new Cameron was a party beast, fearless and eager to try new things. He would be fine in a city with a population of 150,000 people.

The loudspeaker dinged. "Ladies and gentlemen, the captain has turned on the fasten seat belt sign as we prepare for our descent to Cairns...."

one

TROY CARSTAIRS MANNED the gangway of *Sail Away* and smiled at the group of boarding Japanese tourists, squinting in the bright sunlight. "Hi. Welcome aboard. Head on up those stairs"—he pointed, aware of a potential language barrier—"and help yourselves to some breakfast."

The tourists smiled and nodded and headed for the stairs. He didn't know how much they'd understood, but smiles and gestures were his linguistic mainstay. His partner, Jake, kept telling him to take a crash course in a couple of the main tourist languages, but enough of his crew members were bilingual for him to get by.

The couple coming up the gangway now sounded British, or at least the woman complaining about the "ungodly hour" did. Troy swallowed a laugh. It was eight, not five.

"Good morning," he greeted.

"Hello." The man extended a hand, and Troy shook it. "Can you tell us, is it safe to go out on the water today? My wife is worried about the weather." The man, tall, gray-haired, and dressed in the far-north Queensland uniform of shorts and T-shirt, put his arm around the ungodly-hour woman, who glared at Troy, her scowl pronounced. Troy had seen that scowl before. It was the I'm-doing-this-because-I-have-to-and-will-come-up-with-any-excuse-possible-to-get-out-of-it scowl. She was probably a habitually early riser and didn't give a crap about the weather.

He gave his best beach-bum smile and turned back to the man. "The weather today is perfect for being on the water. Hardly any wind, no chop. It's going to be a glorious day."

Mrs. Ungodly-hour's frown intensified. "What about those?" She waved an arm at the bank of dark clouds hovering inland.

"Nothing to worry about. You're in the tropics here, ma'am, and it's November. We generally get a little shower every afternoon, but by the time that blows across to us, we'll be on our way back in." He winked at her and loved the way she flushed purple. "You'll probably appreciate the rain after the heat today. It's going to be a hot one." Which was kind of obvious, with the sun already beating down, the air thick with humidity.

Her husband smiled. "See, darling? Nothing to worry about."

The woman's laser-like glare should have incinerated Troy. "You're absolutely certain? Because if something goes wrong, I will sue this company, and I'll be sure to let your employer know it's your fault."

"Darling." Her husband frowned, but Troy held up a hand.

"I'm absolutely certain, ma'am, and as this is my company, you can believe that I would not risk my boat, my customers, or my reputation." Thank God Jake wasn't aboard this morning. He'd have strangled the woman. *Mmm.* He did so love it when Jake was masterful.

"Thank you very much." The man's smile was slightly forced as he hustled his wife onto the boat.

"No problem." Troy's cheeks ached from his own forced smile. "If you go up those stairs, we have a continental breakfast laid out on the upper deck." He turned back to the gangway to meet the next passenger, and a weird sexual shock, the kind he only felt when he was with Jake, shuddered down his spine.

The man walking toward him wore cargo shorts and a polo shirt, very similar to the uniform Troy and Jake required of their staff. The difference was, where their staff were, as a rule, sun-browned, sleekly muscled, and fit, this man's pasty white skin and lanky, awkward stature instantly labeled him as an office drone of some sort. He was kind of cute, in an indoors, geeky way, but not at all Troy's type.

"Hi," Troy didn't have to force his smile this time. "Welcome aboard."

"Thanks," the man mumbled with a distinctly American accent. He had a lost air, and Troy pegged him for the type who planned on an adventure holiday in Australia, then arrived and realized that adventure was harder than it looked on TV. Most of them decided on a Great Barrier Reef snorkel and scuba cruise instead.

It was how he and Jake made most of their money. Easy money, too, since those guys inevitably chickened out and stayed safe and dry on the pontoon. Still, he always felt kind of sorry for them.

"I'm Troy Carstairs." He offered his hand. The man gave

him a vaguely startled glance, then took his hand. Heat rushed through Troy, and a sheen of sweat that had nothing to do with the morning sun broke out on his upper lip. *What the hell?*

"Cameron Hall."

Troy let go of the man's hand with some relief. "Well, Cameron, if you head up those stairs, we've laid out a complimentary breakfast on the upper deck. We'll be underway in the next forty minutes or so." He was pretty sure that Cameron would grab a plate of food, settle into a corner of the deck, and stay there all the way out to the pontoon. It was a shame, because the guy seemed lonely and could probably do with some socialization.

"Right. Thanks."

Troy watched him go. Despite the obvious *keep away* signals and overwhelming geekiness, there was something strangely appealing about Cameron Hall.

Cameron helped himself to toast and fruit and wished again he'd just stayed home in New York. Coming to Australia to *reinvent* himself was the dumbest idea he'd ever had. He looked around for a seat. There was an empty row next to the cabin door, shaded from the blinding sun and out of the way. Cameron started in that direction, then deliberately stopped. Reinventing himself may have been a dumb idea, but he was here now and there was no point wasting a two-hundred-dollar reef cruise with a corner seat.

He returned to the buffet table and picked out a couple of pastries. Screw being healthy. He was on vacation, right?

He marched over to a seat near the rail, right next to a boisterous group of teenagers. They glanced at him briefly and then resumed their conversation. Cameron picked at his breakfast and wished he had the confidence to take off his shirt like so many of the locals and tourists. Even at eight in the morning, the sun was blisteringly hot and the humidity almost unbearable.

Speaking of the sun.... He put his plate down and dug into his bag for sunblock. He'd been warned over and over that the Australian sun was vicious, and the last thing he needed was sunburn. As it was, he was practically blinded by the glare off the water.

He'd just finished slathering himself when the boat jerked and pulled slowly away from the pier. He picked at his breakfast and breathed deeply. The boat picked up speed, and the breeze blew salt spray into his face.

It was fantastic.

Cameron tipped his head back and propped his feet on the bottom rung of the rail. The sun soaked into him, the spray kept it from being too hot, and for the first time since his arrival, he relaxed.

A shadow fell over his face, and he opened his eyes. A tall man stood in his sun, and Cameron sat up, suddenly aware that the teenagers were gone. Had he fallen asleep?

"Hi." The man who'd welcomed him to the boat sat in the vacant chair next to him, a clipboard dangling from his hand. "Sorry I woke you."

Cameron rubbed his eyes. "No problem. I guess I drifted off."

"Are you wearing sunscreen? Out on the water, UV is intensified."

"Yeah, the pharmacist said that. He recommended

this." Cameron fished the tube out of his bag and showed the man—Troy?

"That's a good one." Troy smiled, intensifying his laugh lines, and a disturbing frisson of pleasure skittered down Cameron's spine. "So, you should be set. Now, have you ever been out on one of these cruises before?"

"No." Cameron shook his head. Troy had really nice eyes, like milk chocolate. He didn't normally notice stuff like that.

"Okay, so we're headed to the Sail Away pontoon. It's about two hours out from Cairns. The pontoon has an underwater observatory and a glass-bottomed boat that makes regular trips around the reef. We also have a life-guard-supervised area for snorkeling. The weather's been excellent the past few days, so visibility on the reef is going to be awesome."

Relief bloomed in Cameron's chest. He could deal with an underwater observatory and glass-bottomed boat. And snorkeling was really just floating face-down and breathing through a tube, right? He could do that. Especially with a lifeguard watching. "What kind of stuff is there to see on the reef?"

Troy grinned broadly. "Everything. The sun's shining, so the colors will be really bright. There are a dozen or so species of fish in all different sizes that live on this reef and heaps of coral. Some of the fish are practically tame. They know we'll feed them, so they flock to us."

Troy gestured enthusiastically, and Cameron's gaze fixed on the large brown hands and muscled forearms.

God, what was wrong with him? He pulled himself together and smiled. "It sounds good. Fun."

"It is fun. A lot of people are surprised when they touch the fish. They don't feel slimy at all, just kind of soft."

Cameron blinked. "You can touch the fish?" That sounded pretty cool. It'd be great to go home and tell people he'd touched tropical fish at the Great Barrier Reef.

"Yeah, of course. It's harder if you're just snorkeling, but we have this helmet walk...." Troy held out his clipboard and pointed at a photo of someone wearing a space-suit style helmet, complete with oxygen line. "Basically, you put on the helmet and we fill it with air. The air bubble stops water from getting in and lets you breathe normally. There's a platform under the pontoon, and we take you down there. The fish will come to you."

Only half-listening, Cameron pointed at the other picture on the page. "What's this?"

Troy hesitated. "That's scuba diving."

"So I could go to the fish, instead of waiting for them to come to me?"

"Yes, although we do ask our divers to stay within a certain area."

"Does it matter that I've never done it before?" The hair on his arms stood on end.

Troy shook his head. "All our staff are certified scuba instructors. Can you swim?"

Cameron snorted. "Believe me, if I couldn't swim, there's no way in hell I'd be on a boat." He studied the photo again. "So I put on the tank and the mask and basically just swim underwater?"

The grin flashed again. "It's a bit more complicated than that, but basically, yes."

Determination flared. "Sign me up."

"Sure." Troy sounded reluctant but dutifully wrote Cameron's name on the list, then detached a sheet of paper from the back of the clipboard. "You need to sign this form. Are you on any medications?"

"No." Cameron scanned the form. It was a basic indemnity waiver. He held out his hand for the pen. Troy gave it to him, and their hands brushed.

Cameron jerked back. "Sorry. Electric shock." His face grew hot, and he concentrated on filling out the form. Stupid to be embarrassed. Electric shocks happened all the time.

"No worries." Troy took the pen and form back. "When we get to the pontoon, head to the back where the scuba equipment is. You can change your mind at any time, even after we're in the water."

"I won't change my mind." He was going to swim with the fishes.

Troy watched Cameron stroke tentatively through the water. He'd been surprised when the Yank had actually turned up for the scuba lesson. Surprised enough to take the class himself, when he normally let one of his crew do it.

Cameron had continued to surprise him as they went through all the preliminary steps, through the first moments in the water. He'd appeared nervous when Troy had explained the need for equalizing, and downright terrified when the subject of stingers came up. The offer of skinsuits had dialed it down a bit, but Troy was still impressed that he hadn't backed out. A lot of people did at the mention of jellyfish.

As the small group drifted around the base of the pontoon, Troy kept a watchful eye on them all, offering supportive gestures when necessary. Cameron was a natural. He swam slowly among the fish, clearly determined to get the most out of this experience. The man's surprising grace was shockingly arousing, and Troy dragged his attention away. Weird.

He turned his focus to some of the other divers. One of the teenage boys—as usual, the one who'd been the most vocal during the pre-dive lesson—showed distinct signs of panic. Troy swam over and put a hand on his arm. The whites of his eyes were showing. Slowly, using the hand signals he'd painstakingly taught the group, Troy asked if the boy wanted to go back. The immediate, heartfelt nod was answer enough.

Signaling the other supervisor, Troy indicated that he was going up. It was tough keeping the panicky teen calm enough to stop and equalize regularly, but eventually they were back on the pontoon. The boy ripped off his mask, gasping hard enough that Troy worried he'd hyperventilate. "You okay, man? Take deep breaths. Slowly. In, out. There you go."

The boy slowly calmed down, and finally gave Troy a shaky smile. "I'm good. Thanks. Sorry about..." He waved a hand toward the water.

Troy smiled back. "No worries. Happens all the time. It's scary if you're not used to it." And yet nervous Cameron took to it like—well, like a fish to water.

Cameron unstrapped the oxygen tank and let the equipment guy help him take it off. Energy zinged through him. He'd swum with fish. Touching them had been so cool, and one of the instructors had taken his picture with one of those underwater cameras.

This was why he'd come to Australia. In the water, with

the fish and the coral and the amazing quiet, he didn't feel geeky. He was powerful. Strong.

"How'd it go?"

He glanced up and met Troy's melted milk chocolate gaze. The other man smiled, and Cameron smiled back, for some reason suddenly breathless. "It was fantastic. Can I go back in after lunch?"

"Absolutely. Someone will be taking a group down at about two. It'll just be a short dive, though, because we leave at three-thirty."

"Okay." He hesitated. "So, uh, do you guys offer scuba lessons? So I could go by myself?"

"You should never go down without a buddy."

Cameron flushed hot and felt ridiculous. He knew Troy hadn't meant that sexually, but an image flashed through his mind of himself kneeling before Troy as he leaned against the rail at the back of the pontoon. It was stupid. He wasn't into men.

Troy was talking, and Cameron forced himself to focus. "...get your dive certificate, you mean? Sorry, the only lessons we give are the day-trip ones."

"Oh." *I'm not disappointed.* There was no reason to be disappointed. There were probably dozens of companies in Cairns that offered lessons. He'd just try one of them. "Could you recommend someone who does?"

Troy shrugged. "Sure. I'll get you a list when we get back." He paused. "Although..." Another hesitation. "Look, we could work something out. You could come on a couple of trips, and I'll give you lessons. Get you certified."

Yes! Cameron's chest expanded with sheer pleasure. "That would be great. I mean..." He cleared his throat. Way to sound like a geek. "I mean, that would be really cool. Thanks." He couldn't help the grin.

Troy grinned back, and Cameron's stomach flipped. "No problem. Listen, we'll sort it out back in Cairns. Obviously, we won't charge the full trip fee. I'll talk to Jake. He handles most of that stuff."

"Jake?" Cameron looked around. None of the staff had been introduced as Jake.

"My partner. He and I usually take turns coming out on the boat so one of us can be in the office."

"Oh. Okay." Something about the expression on Troy's face when he said *partner... Get over it, Cameron.* Why couldn't he stop thinking of Troy in a sexual sense?

What the hell is wrong with me? Troy signaled Katy to start serving lunch. They didn't give dive certificate lessons. He and Jake had talked about it, but in the end it was something they'd tabled for the future, deciding to focus on tourists who were purely out for a day of fun. And yet, when he'd seen the expression on Cameron's face, he'd blurted the offer.

Jake was going to think he was nuts.

There was just something about Cameron, though. Even the thought made him feel vaguely disloyal to Jake, which was stupid. He'd been attracted to other men before. It was normal. It didn't change the fact that he was completely and totally committed to his boyfriend. Besides, he wasn't really attracted to Cameron.

Was he? With only a few hours in the sun, the other man's pasty skin had taken on a faint golden tinge, the indoor pallor gone. In the water, he'd been utterly graceful. And while they were talking, the warm air had begun to dry Cameron's hair, and Troy's fingers had itched to stroke through the salt-damp curls. In fact, Cameron kind of reminded Troy of Jake, even though the two men couldn't be further apart in looks or personality.

Troy shook his head. He was probably just hungry. Breakfast was a long time ago. And maybe horny. Tonight, he'd jump Jake and forget all about Cameron.

two

THE BELL over the door dinged, and Jake glanced up from the computer. Any distraction from the bookkeeping was welcome. He smiled at Troy. Was it that time already?

"Hey," his guy said, crossing the room and leaning across the desk. Jake met him halfway, planting a quick, hard kiss on those soft lips. A sharply indrawn breath drew his attention to the man who'd followed Troy into the office.

"Hey, yourself." Jake pulled back and nodded to the stranger. "Going to introduce me to your friend?"

Troy half-turned. "Sure. Jake Paulson, Cameron Hall. Cameron came out to the pontoon with us today, and now he wants to get his dive certificate."

Jake reached for the drawer where they kept the list of reputable dive instructors. "No problem. We have a list of some excellent dive companies. I'll make a copy for you."

Troy cleared his throat and looked away. "Actually, I said we'd give him the lessons."

Jake's hand froze on the drawer handle. *What the hell?*

"Oh." He raised an eyebrow, but Troy's gaze was fixed on the desk. "Okay. Um, what arrangement did you make?"

They didn't do certification lessons. He studied the stranger—Cameron. He was kind of gangly and had a very faint tan, probably as a result of the day on the water. His hair was the same shade between blond and brown as Troy's, but Troy spent so much time outdoors that the sun had streaked his with gold.

Cameron fiddled with his watch. "Troy said you'd work that out."

"Did he?" Jake glanced at Troy, who made a sheepish face.

"Yeah. Uh, I thought he could come out on the boat with the regular day-trippers, and you or I could do his lessons. At a reasonable rate?" The questioning lift to his last sentence was accompanied by his puppy-dog look, the one Jake could never resist.

His gaze met Troy's gorgeous brown one, and his stomach did its usual flip. He sighed. "Sure. Sit down, Cameron, and we'll work something out."

Troy grinned, shooting him a grateful look, and the hairs on the back of Jake's neck stood on end. Why did this matter so much to Troy? He turned his attention back to Cameron as the man sat in one of the visitor's chairs. Cameron's hazel eyes gazed back at him.

"So, I'll leave you two to it." Troy put a hand on Cameron's shoulder and squeezed, and a shock ran down Jake's spine. Troy was a hands-on person, but... His boyfriend smiled at him, and he forced himself to smile back. He was being ridiculous. He had no reason to be jealous. Troy was being nice to a tourist; that was all.

☀

Jake waved goodbye to their latest customer. They'd had a steady stream since Cameron had left, and this was the first time the office had been empty for an hour.

Troy poked his head out the back room where Jake had sent him to do the bookkeeping. "Hey, Jake, can you come back here?"

Jake got up from the stool behind the cash register, followed Troy through the doorway, and was slammed back against the wall. "What—"

Troy's hot mouth slammed against his, soft lips cushioning the impact, his warm, wet tongue probing for entrance.

Mmm. Jake raised his hands and threaded them through Troy's hair, lightly scratching his scalp in the way that drove Troy wild. Troy rewarded him with a groan and pressed his hips into his. Jake's dick rose to meet the hard ridge in Troy's shorts, and he shifted to rub against his lover.

Troy broke the kiss, panting. "Want you."

"I can tell." Jake slid a hand between them, stroked Troy's cock, and squeezed gently. Troy's breath expelled on a gasp, teasing Jake's cheek. "Condom?"

Troy held up a foil package, along with the tube of lube they kept for office *emergencies*. Jake grinned edgily and took the items. "Strip."

Troy yanked off his T-shirt and attacked the buttons of his shorts. Jake liked Troy naked when they fucked, liked to run his hands over Troy's chest. He undid his own shorts, rolled on the condom, then opened the lube and applied it to his fingers as Troy finished stripping and hopped up on the desk. He lay back, bent his knees, and planted his feet. His cock stood at attention, and Jake leaned over to lick the bead of cum leaking from the tip. The salty-sweet flavor drove him wild.

"Mmm." Jake wrapped one hand around Troy's dick, firmly, and trailed the other down, across his balls and over his perineum to circle his hole. Jake's dick throbbed at the sound of Troy's groan. He leaned over Troy and muffled the sound with a kiss as he slid one lubed finger inside.

Troy bit down on Jake's lip and moaned, his muscles tightening around Jake's finger. A second digit joined the first, and Jake moved them slightly. Troy's hips pumped, and his dick, pressed between their bellies, left a wet trail of precum over Jake's skin. Jake loved the way Troy reacted to being touched. He wished he had a dozen hands, so he could touch Troy all over, all at once—his dick, his balls, his hole, his nipples, that soft spot behind his ear that begged for kissing.

An image of Troy propped between the legs of another man filtered through his mind. A gangly, pale-skinned man, Cameron, reclined against Troy's chest, writhing on Jake's fingers in his ass while Cameron stroked his cock and tweaked his nipples... Troy's hand snaked between them and grabbed Jake's cock, stroking almost roughly...

And the image vanished. Jake's balls tightened. Jesus, how could he be turned on by Cameron when he was jealous of Troy's reaction—real or imagined—to him? "Neither of us is going to last long," he huffed, and Troy squeezed Jake's dick.

"Don't care. Put it in." Troy let go, and Jake slid his fingers out and pressed the head of his dick against Troy's hole. First, the ring of resistance, then he was in, sliding into that narrow passage, the muscles tight around him.

Troy groaned. "Jake, move."

Jake withdrew slightly then lunged forward, taking

advantage of the moment to kiss his lover's soft lips and plunge his tongue into the hot, wet warmth of his mouth. Troy's breaths huffed against him, and Jake pulled back and thrust again, and then again, his balls drawing up.

The bell over the outside door dinged.

He glanced over his shoulder. The door to the back room was open, but the desk was situated off to the side. Unless someone stood in the doorway, they wouldn't be seen.

He thrust again.

"Hello? Is anyone here?"

"I'll be just a minute." Jake fought to keep his voice even. He slapped a hand over Troy's mouth—his boyfriend had a tendency to be loud when he came—and reached between them to encircle Troy's cock with his hand. Sweat beaded on Troy's forehead, and from the mindless haze in those melted-chocolate eyes, Jake knew it wouldn't take much to push him over the edge.

He surged forward again, stroking Troy's dick at the same time. Troy's ass clenched around him, and Jake bit his lip hard, holding back the moan that fought to burst free. He squeezed Troy's cock gently, tickling that sensitive spot underneath. His lungs burned. *Come on.*

Beneath him, Troy tensed, and Jake gasped as vise-like pressure encased him. *Oh, God!*

And then Troy went over, cum spurting between Jake's fingers, splashing over their bellies. He moved his hand from Troy's mouth, kissed him again, and thrust twice more before he came apart. His semen pumped into the condom, Troy's ass squeezed around him, and he collapsed forward onto his lover.

"Hello?" Footsteps sounded, becoming louder.

"Just a second. Why don't you have a look at the

brochure on the desk?" Jake levered himself up and grabbed a wad of tissues. He pulled out of Troy's ass, stripped off the condom, and quickly cleaned himself. Troy watched, eyes drowsy, and Jake couldn't resist stealing one more kiss as he zipped his shorts. He loved post-sex Troy, all sleepy and sexy.

Running a hand over his hair, he stepped out into the front room, smile in place.

Jake woke covered in sweat, and it had nothing to do with the balmy night. Careful not to wake Troy, he slid out of bed and headed for the kitchen. Standing in the glow from the window, he drank two glasses of water in quick succession and tried not to think about his dream.

Cameron and Troy knelt on the bed before him, both naked, their bodies different but equally arousing. Jake reached out and stroked his hands over their chests, loving the way Cam shivered and Troy leaned into his touch. Without him having to say a word, Troy propped himself against the headboard and Cam settled between his legs, facing him. Jake climbed onto the bed with them, caught Cam's chin in his hand and turned his face for a kiss. His lips were warm and soft, and he tasted so good.

Jake's cock was enveloped by a warm, capable hand, and he pulled back to watch Troy stroke him. Cam, not to be outdone, leaned down and enclosed Troy's dick in his mouth. Jake sucked in a deep breath as Cam's head bobbed over Troy's lap and the part of Troy's cock that was still exposed glistened with saliva.

"Jake?"

He looked up and met Troy's gaze. His lover was smiling, his cheeks already flushed with passion.

"Look at him." Troy gestured to Cameron, to the curve of his back. "Isn't he beautiful?"

Jake took in the sight and moved away from Troy's stroking hand. He arranged himself behind Cam and slid a single finger into Cam's ass. His body jerked, and Jake wriggled the finger until he relaxed, then slowly added another.

That was when he'd woken up. It was just a dream. It meant nothing. He hadn't dreamed of another man since he met Troy—well, except for Chris Hemsworth, and that didn't count.

It was probably because he'd been so stupidly jealous that afternoon. That's the only reason he'd dream of Cameron in bed with Troy. And he was there because... maybe because that way he was cheating, too?

It made no sense. Still, it was just a dream. So why was he disappointed to wake up?

three

"THANKS FOR SORTING out that stuff for Cameron yesterday." Troy finished stacking their breakfast dishes in the dishwasher. "I don't know what got into me, but the lessons will probably be fun. And, you know, a trial run if we decide to do them later." He turned to where Jake sat at the kitchen table, tying his shoe.

"Yeah, no problem."

Troy frowned. Something was bothering Jake, and damned if he knew what. He hated seeing his boyfriend like this, all quiet and withdrawn. "Hey, why don't you go out today? I can man the office." He cringed. He hated the office and only took his turn in there because Jake hated it too.

Jake gazed at him, one of his dark eyebrows arched. "It's still my turn."

Troy shrugged. "I know, but you seem kind of off-balance. It won't hurt for us to swap."

Jake stood, grinning, and took Troy in his arms. "I love you." Jake kissed him, slow and hot, their tongues tangling. Jake's hands tugged his T-shirt up, and then long fingers stroked Troy's chest, pausing to tease his nipples. Troy jerked away, panting.

"Stop. We'll be late." He knew Jake, and when Jake stroked his chest, it was a clear sign that he wanted to get naked.

Jake laughed, and the happy sound lightened Troy's heart. "Okay, so we'll take a rain check. But," Jake backed toward the kitchen door, "I say we close the office and both go out today."

Troy blinked. "Really? We haven't done that for ages." They managed to sneak in the odd trip out on their personal boat, but they hadn't both been on the cruise boat at the same time since... was it two years?

Jake was watching him, expression strangely guarded again.

Nuh-uh. I want happy Jake back. "Let's do it." Troy smiled. "And maybe while everyone's having lunch, we can talk about that rain check."

Cameron approached the boat, hands shaking with nerves. *Don't be stupid, don't be stupid.* He was sweating, and not just from the already oppressive heat. It was ridiculous to be nervous. Especially because it wasn't diving he was nervous about.

Meeting Jake the day before had been a revelation. First, his instincts were right—Troy was gay. But Jake himself— wow. And that was the scary part. He'd never thought *wow* about a man in his entire life. Even if he was into men— which he wasn't—he didn't think he'd be attracted to the serious, broody type. No, he'd be more likely to go for the sunny-personality type—like Troy.

Stop it! It was all irrelevant. He liked women. He'd been with women, so he had to be straight. And Troy and Jake were a couple, anyway.

Cameron walked up the gangway, stopping short halfway. Where he'd expected to see Troy greeting customers, Jake stood, dark hair gleaming in the hot sun.

Someone cleared their throat, and Cameron realized he was blocking traffic. He hurried the rest of the way on board the boat and edged to the side so Jake could direct the tourists upstairs to breakfast.

"Welcome back." Jake smiled at him, and the dimple Cameron had noticed yesterday flashed.

"Hi." His voice sounded breathless, and he coughed. "Uh, I guess Troy's in the office today?"

Jake's smile dimmed slightly, and his eyes narrowed. "No, he's upstairs supervising the buffet. We decided to close the office for the day."

"Oh." Cameron swallowed. They were both on the boat. "Are you going to dive, too?"

"Probably." Jake's gaze fixed over Cameron's shoulder, and he smiled professionally. "Welcome aboard," he said, and Cameron jerked his head around to see a couple standing at the top of the gangway. He hadn't even heard them.

While Jake answered their questions, Cameron slipped away and climbed the steps to the upper deck. Breakfast was set out, just like yesterday. He grabbed a plate and filled it with pastries and fruit.

"Try the mango. It's really sweet today." He jumped at the sound of Troy's voice. The other man stood beside him, grinning.

"Hi." Cameron jerked his gaze from those melted-chocolate eyes. "Uh, I saw Jake downstairs." He took some mango, more because it gave him something to do than because he wanted it.

"Yeah, isn't it great? We hardly ever both go out to the pontoon." Troy took hold of Cameron's elbow, and tingles shot up his arm. He tried not to stumble as Troy steered him toward the empty seats by the rail. "It was different when we first started the company, you know? We had a much smaller boat and a really small crew, so we both had to be on the water. We got to spend the whole day together, even if we were working." Troy propped his feet on the lower rung of the railing. "Now we only see each other at night." He flicked a glance at Cameron. "Working weekends is a bitch."

Cameron swallowed dryly and fished for something intelligent to say. "Do you work every weekend?"

Troy stole a piece of melon from his plate. "We used to, but we have enough senior crew now that we take one weekend a month off. And we each rotate a day off during the week. It still sucks, though."

"What sucks is that I'm working while you sit on your ass eating and complaining." Jake's words were belied by his mild tone and half-smile.

Troy's habitual grin reappeared. "Nag, nag, nag." He stood. "I'll see you later, Cameron."

"Yeah. See you." Cameron watched them both go. They walked close together, almost touching but not quite. An image rose before Cameron of Jake slowly running a hand from Troy's wrist, up his bare arm to his shoulder, down over the tanned, sweat-dampened muscles of his chest. Troy shivered, and Jake's dark head descended—

He yanked himself out of the fantasy. Dear God, what was happening to him? He wasn't into men. He'd been with women. His relationship with Tamara had lasted nearly a year. He *liked* having sex with women. Besides, if he were gay, or bi—which could *maybe* be possible—wasn't that something he should've known by now?

Jake swam lazily, trying to keep watch over the dive group slowly drifting through the water, but his gaze was irresistibly drawn to Troy and Cameron. Their movements were almost sinuous, and even underwater his cock was hardening. All he could think of was Troy, lying back against Cameron's chest while the American played with his body.

He forced his attention back to the divers swimming slowly amid the brightly colored tropical fish. They were a good group, competent and sensible, and they were clearly enjoying themselves. His gaze drifted back to his boyfriend just in time to see Troy put his hand on Cameron's arm and gesture toward the underside of the pontoon.

Electric shocks exploded down Jake's spine at the sight of Troy's hand on the other man, and his cock throbbed painfully. Damn if his jealousy hadn't turned to lust. He wanted to swim over to them, to push Cameron up against Troy and grind himself into the man's ass. To kiss Troy while Cameron was sandwiched between them. What would Troy say about that? They'd never discussed a threesome—in fact, it wasn't something he'd ever thought about.

He jerked himself around in the water so he could no longer see them and joined the tourists he was supposed to be supervising. Thank God the water was warm enough to forgo wetsuits. His boardshorts were loose enough to hide his erection.

While they were in the water, at least.

Troy propped his dive tank against the bench and turned to see Cameron struggling to get his off.

"Here, let me help." He crossed swiftly to stand behind the other man. "It helps a bit if the weight isn't on the straps." He lifted the tank, taking its weight into his hands, and heard the distinctive snick as the straps came undone. Cameron turned, presumably to take the tank, and the back of Troy's hand brushed Cameron's shoulder.

They both froze. Awareness zinged through Troy, and his mouth went dry. Over Cameron's shoulder, his gaze clashed with Jake's.

"Go to lunch." He almost didn't recognize his own voice.

Cameron backed away. "Sure. I'll..." He didn't finish the sentence, swiftly retreating to the main part of the pontoon.

Troy put down the tank, and when he looked up again, Jake was beside him.

"Come on." Jake grabbed his arm and yanked him toward the stairs leading to the underwater observatory. "I want that rain check."

They raced down the slippery steps faster than was safe. Troy twisted his arm free the second they got to the bottom, and wrapped his arm around Jake's waist, yanking him close. Their bodies, still damp from the sea, collided at the same time their mouths meshed together.

Jake's hand dragged down Troy's chest, and Troy yanked his head back. "Jake," he gasped. "Need to talk."

"No." Jake guided Troy's mouth back to his. "Need you," he muttered against Troy's lips.

Troy welcomed the hot slide of his lover's tongue and lost himself in shared exploration of each other's mouths.

Jake laid kisses along the line of Troy's jaw, tracking a hot, moist path to his ear. He sucked Troy's earlobe into his mouth, nipping it sharply, and then pulled back. "You're right." He sucked in a deep breath, panting. Their gazes met. "We need to talk."

"I think…" Troy swallowed. God, what if Jake didn't understand? "I'm a little bit attracted to Cameron." He closed his eyes, then snapped them open, unwilling to miss Jake's response.

Which was a tiny smile. "Babe, I want to fuck him while he sucks your cock."

Lust punched in Troy's stomach. Jake's blunt words hovered in the air. Troy drew a cautious breath. "We've never…"

Jake let him go and ran a hand through his hair. "I know. And I never thought we would. You've always been enough for me. You *are* enough for me. I just… I watched you touching him, and I want to sandwich him between us and bite him."

A shudder chased down Troy's spine, and Jake smiled, dimple flashing. "You like that, don't you?"

"Yeah," Troy confessed on a long exhale, adjusting his hard-on in his shorts. "Do we… I mean…"

"Should we go for it? I don't know. I love you, and I don't ever want anything to come between us."

"Me either. But…."

"Yeah, I want to, too. Reckon he'd be up for it?"

Troy's excitement vanished, and his stomach sank. "I think he's straight."

Jake drew him closer and pressed their foreheads together. This close, their breaths mingled. "He thinks he's straight, anyway. But the way he looks at you..." Jake leaned in that last little bit and kissed Troy. "In the meantime..."

He gently pushed at Troy's chest until Troy stepped back and leaned against the cool glass window that showcased the reef beyond. Jake nibbled his way down Troy's neck, stopping briefly to suck the skin where his pulse beat. Lust curled in Troy's stomach, and he raised his hand to grip the back of Jake's neck. Damp, silky dark hair brushed his fingers as Jake licked his way down to Troy's left nipple. He drew it into his mouth, sucking hard. A groan was torn from Troy's throat, and he thrust his hips forward, his dick rubbing against Jake's chest.

Jake pulled back and licked his lips. "Mmm. Salty." He dropped to his knees and carefully freed Troy's erection from his shorts. Jake feathered kisses over the painfully swollen shaft, licked the drop of pre-cum from the tip, and then opened his mouth wide and took him deep.

Troy tipped his head back as hot, wet heaven enveloped him.

Cameron stood frozen at the bottom of the stairs. He couldn't tear his gaze away as Jake sucked Troy's cock.

He'd wanted somewhere quiet to think about the crazy, intense attraction he felt for both Troy *and* Jake. He hadn't expected this. He could hardly breathe, and his dick was harder than it had ever been before. Which maybe answered some of his questions.

Troy groaned, his hips jerking. Jake's hands were on the backs of Troy's thighs, massaging, and as Cameron watched, one slid up to Troy's ass. Cameron couldn't see what Jake did, but whatever it was made Troy cry out sharply and Cameron's cock throb painfully.

Abruptly, Troy's head rolled to the side and his eyes opened. His gorgeous milk-chocolate eyes were dilated, dreamy, and Cameron's stomach clenched with desire.

Troy let go of Jake's head and reached out to Cameron. "Join us." His voice was thick.

For an endless second, Cameron wavered. Then Troy's eyes slid closed again, and he cried out, his face tightening as orgasm overtook him.

Cameron turned and ran.

four

JAKE STOOD in the cabin doorway and watched Cameron. The man sat on the deck with his back against the rail, head tipped back, eyes closed.

Troy came and stood beside Jake. "Have you spoken to him?"

Jake shook his head. "You?"

"Not since we left the pontoon. And even then, it was all dive stuff. I screwed up. He's really freaked out."

Jake shifted his weight. "Okay. So, we try again. Let's keep it casual." He strode across the deck and dropped to sit beside Cameron. Seconds later, Troy joined them.

"Hey, Cam." Jake hoped he was the only one who heard the tremor in his voice.

Cameron opened his eyes, and his face blanked. "Hi."

Jake's stomach sank. Not an auspicious beginning.

"So, uh, how long are you here for?" Next to him, Troy coughed and nudged him. Yeah, he sounded inane, but Troy wasn't exactly jumping in with brilliant conversation starters, either.

"My return flight isn't until the end of January. I'm not

sure yet if I'll stay here or travel around a bit." Cameron didn't look at either of them, his gaze focused on the deck.

"When did you arrive?" *Thank you, Troy!* The tension in Jake's shoulders loosened slightly as his boyfriend picked up the conversational ball.

"Friday."

Jake blinked. "You've only been here a couple days?"

"Have you had a chance to do any sightseeing? Aside from the reef." Troy's voice had that excited edge it got when he had an idea. Jake crossed his fingers and watched Cameron's face carefully. He itched to smooth back that lock of hair that kept flopping onto the man's forehead.

"No. I meant to, but I'd rather do the diving lessons first." It seemed that he was going to say something else. Maybe he wanted to cancel the lessons?

"Great." Troy bulldozed forward, cutting off anything Cameron might have said. "We'll show you around. Ooh, I know—let's go clubbing tonight. I'm revved enough to go dancing."

"Uh, I-I-I don't..." The sheer terror on Cameron's face roused Jake's protective instincts. He laid a hand on Cameron's shoulder.

"It'll be fun, Cam. We won't go anywhere too crazy. Just somewhere we can have a few drinks and talk and dance. No alcohol, either—not if you're diving tomorrow." Beneath his hand, Cameron's muscles knotted and unknotted.

"Okay," Cameron muttered, and Jake squeezed his shoulder and drew his hand back.

"Awesome. Listen, it'll probably be easiest if you meet us at our place. It's only five minutes from the Esplanade, and we can take the car from there." Troy fished one of the company pens from his shorts pocket and grabbed

Cameron's hand. He wrote the address on the back, then turned it over and drew a map on the palm, explaining directions as he scrawled.

Cameron watched the pen move, his expression half-fascinated, half-startled, and possessive lust surged in Jake's chest. *Mine. Both of them.*

Cameron didn't know what the hell had possessed him. Why had he agreed to go out with Troy and Jake? It was... it was... it was just plain dumb. He'd just figured out how incredibly attracted he was to them both, and then he'd seen Jake sucking Troy—the most incredibly arousing thing he'd ever seen—and he'd decided to avoid them both as much as possible. No more casual conversation. He'd be really careful not to touch either of them.

It seemed like he really might be gay, or bi, or whatever, which was really weird because he'd never had thoughts in that direction before. He really needed to spend some time online doing research. Lots of research. But just thinking about Jake and Troy together, and maybe him too... No, he definitely couldn't just hang out with them. He'd just take the dive lessons and then say goodbye.

Although, he could take the lessons with another company, but wasn't that a bit cowardly? He was a mature adult. What kind of weenie would he be if he couldn't deal with a bit of sexual attraction?

Then Jake and Troy had sat next to him, and Jake had called him *Cam* in that sexy voice, and he'd been incredibly glad that his upraised knees hid his erection. He thought maybe they were a bit uncomfortable, but then Troy had insisted they go out—dancing, of all things, like he didn't have two left feet—and Jake had called him Cam again, and he'd agreed.

Cameron studied his hand. He'd carefully transcribed Troy's directions and map onto paper when he arrived back at the hotel, but some of the faded ink smears still remained. Who would have guessed his palm was an erogenous zone? His entire hand was still tingling from Troy's touch.

Jake and Troy's house was set back from the road with a lush, tropical garden shading the front windows. Cameron turned onto the front path and sucked in a deep breath. The new, reinvented Cameron could handle a night of dancing with new friends.

The front door was open, with only the screen protecting the entrance. He knocked.

"It's open!" Troy sounded out of breath.

Cameron opened the door and stepped into the house. The tiny entrance nook opened into a nice-sized living area on the right and a corridor on the left, lined with doorways. Even as he hesitated, Troy hurried into the corridor from one of the rooms.

"Hey. You're right on time. Jake's nearly ready." Troy's face was flushed, his mouth swollen and red, and like a slap, Cameron realized that they'd been having sex. His gaze fixed on Troy's pouty lips, and his balls tightened. Were they puffy from kisses or...?

"Okay, are we ready?" Jake strode down the hall. He, too, was slightly flushed. "Let's go."

Cameron avoided Jake's gaze and turned toward the door. Was it wrong that he was getting hard, thinking about Troy and Jake having sex? God, how was he going to get through a night without saying or doing something stupid? *A couple of hours and you can go. Just a couple of hours.*

Troy leaned against the bar, his gaze focused on Cameron. The other man stood straight, no slouching or casual leaning, and gripped his soda so tightly his knuckles were white. Why he was so nervous, Troy didn't know. Well, actually, that wasn't true. Cameron was nervous because Troy had invited him to join in while Jake sucked his dick, and then Cameron had arrived at their house when he and Jake were very obviously experiencing post-fuck glow.

The nervousness actually reassured Troy. Cameron was attracted to him and Jake. Troy knew it. And the fact that he was so skittish just meant that they had to make the first move.

Next to him, Jake ran a hand over Troy's hip and squeezed. Taking the hint, Troy put his bottle down on the bar and straightened. "Come on, Cam. Let's dance."

He grabbed Cameron's wrist before the man could protest and towed him out to the dance floor. He'd noticed earlier that Cameron wavered when Jake called him Cam. Troy wasn't above taking advantage of that.

"I can't dance," Cameron half-shouted over the rhythmic beat of the music.

Troy shook his head, pretending he couldn't hear, and led Cameron far enough into the gyrating crowd that escape would be difficult. The throng of people pulsed around them, forcing them closer to each other. Within the press of bodies, there were no personal boundaries and no need for inhibitions. It took only moments for Cameron to relax and go with the music.

Troy let the crowd jostle him up against Cam, and when the other man jolted, Troy shot him a rueful grin and a half-shrug. He could tell from Cameron's occasional jerk that he too was the recipient of the usual groping common in a crowded nightclub. Troy had always considered it a compliment—although he could do without the pinching—and it looked like Cameron was okay with it too.

Soon, they were smashed up so close to each other there was barely an inch between them. Every time the crowd forced Troy against Cameron, he made sure to press his dick, hard and throbbing, along Cam's leg. One particular surge of bodies pressed them together long enough for Troy to realize that Cameron was turned on, too.

He glanced toward the bar, hoping to catch Jake's eye, but the throng of bodies that he'd been so grateful for blocked his view. Instead, he locked gazes with Cameron. The flush on the other man's face could have been from the heat of the club, but the dilated pupils spelled desire. Pure lust skittered down Troy's spine, and he leaned in close enough for their clothes to brush together.

A figure shoved through the horde and came up behind Cameron, crowding him, and Troy broke away from Cameron's gaze to meet Jake's lustful stare.

He lunged forward, trapping Cameron between them, and met his boyfriend's mouth with his own. Jake was hot. Troy could tell, because his tongue plunged right in, dueling with Troy's. Between them, Cameron squirmed, as if trying to escape, and Jake broke the kiss to press his face into the soft skin where Cameron's neck met his shoulder.

Troy noticed the shock on Cameron's face and hurried to speak into his ear. "We want you. We've never done this before. You're the only person we've ever thought of being with." Jake nibbled his way up Cameron's neck toward his earlobe, and from Cameron's shiver, he liked it. Troy knew exactly how he felt, how talented Jake's mouth was. He reached down between his and Cameron's bodies and adjusted his dick in his pants. The back of his hand brushed Cameron's cock, hard and ready, and it jerked.

Troy smiled, slow and sexual.

He turned his hand and rubbed the front of Cameron's jeans. The other man's gasp was lost as Troy captured his mouth in a deep kiss. It was different from kissing Jake, softer and less demanding, but just as intoxicating, and muscles all down his torso tightened. His moan, inaudible over the throb of the music, rumbled through his chest. Jake's hands—nobody else raised that tingle—slid over his flank and squeezed his ass.

Cameron's tongue, until then acquiescent, traced over Troy's teeth. His hips moved, pressing his cock firmly into Troy's hand, begging for attention. Troy stroked and squeezed gently. He fingered the zipper of Cameron's jeans. Could he?

His balls drew up just thinking about it, and he thrust against Cam, pushing him back into Jake. Cam broke their kiss, panting, and Jake raised his head to murmur something in his ear. Cameron flushed, and his chest heaved with deep breaths. Familiar with Jake's preferences, Troy could guess what he'd said.

He glanced around quickly. The crowd provided some measure of privacy, but the last thing they needed was an indecent exposure charge. That would definitely scare off Cameron. His gaze snagged on the dark corridor leading back to the bathrooms. If he remembered right, there were a couple of doors back there marked Staff Only.

Troy turned Cameron so he faced Jake, who took immediate advantage and captured his mouth in a deep kiss. Pressed up against Cameron's back, Troy carefully shuffled the duo through the crowd toward the edge of the dance floor. Their progress was slow, hampered by Jake's refusal to let either of them go, but eventually they broke through the worst of the crowd.

Jake immediately took hold of Cameron's wrist, then looked at Troy and mouthed, "Where?" Troy nudged him in the right direction, and within moments, they were in the dimly lit hall.

Taking the lead, Troy hurried to a door at the end of the corridor and turned the knob. Thankfully, it wasn't locked, and he shoved the door open. Jake and Cameron crowded up behind him as he fumbled for a light switch.

Finally, bright fluorescent light flooded what turned out to be a tiny office, containing a desk, chair, and filing cabinet. Jake closed the door and snicked the lock, then barely paused before he grabbed Cameron and slammed him up against the wall, meshing their mouths together. Troy leaned against the door. He'd never seen Jake kissing anybody, had only ever felt it, but it was just as hot to see his lover's absorption as it was to be on the receiving end. He undid his jeans and freed his dick from his boxers. His cock was already leaking, and a swipe of his thumb smeared the precum over the head as he stroked lightly down his shaft, then back the other way, more firmly.

Jake broke the kiss and bit Cameron's earlobe. Cam's ragged breathing and the way he clutched Jake's shoulders were evidence that, even if he thought he was straight, he had definite leanings.

Troy moved closer while Jake sucked on Cam's ear and reaching around his lover started to undo Cam's shirt. Jake abandoned Cameron's ear and began licking a path down his neck to his chest, following Troy's fingers. Troy skated his nails lightly over Cam's belly, heard the hitch in his breathing and felt his muscles contract. His own dick, hard as nails, was throbbing violently by the time he unfastened Cam's jeans and stood back to let Jake work his magic.

Troy propped himself on the edge of the desk and fisted his cock. Jake's dark head was a shocking contrast to the pale skin of Cameron's stomach. Troy's lover scraped his teeth over Cam's belly, and Cam's hands seized Jake's head pulling him closer. Heavy breaths and ragged gasps filled the air. Troy realized that some were his. He squeezed his cock, then let go and let his hand drift lower and fondled his balls. Jake liked to watch him pleasure himself, sometimes, but he'd never realized how arousing it would be to get himself off while Jake was with another man.

Cameron cried out, and Troy jerked his awareness back to the room. Jake had taken the head of Cam's dick into his mouth. Troy imagined what he was doing, that little tongue-dart into the slit, the sliding lick. Cameron's head fell back as Jake's lunged forward, taking Cameron's cock deep into his throat, and Troy let go of his balls and began pumping his cock in earnest. Jake's head was bobbing as he sucked hard, and Cameron was making these little sounds...

Troy came on a long moan that mingled with Cameron's cry of fulfillment. He forced himself to keep his eyes open, to watch as Jake swallowed every drop of Cam's cum, licked him clean and rose to kiss him.

Cameron slammed the hotel room door and leaned against it. *God, what did I do?* He slid down the door until his ass hit the floor, and then drew up his knees and rested his forehead on them.

Was it cheating if a guy gave you a blow job while his boyfriend watched? And did the fact that his most amazing orgasm ever had been from a man mean that he was definitely bi?

He banged his head back against the door. What the hell was wrong with him? Dragging himself to his feet, Cameron made his way into the bathroom and turned the shower on hot, barely waiting long enough to strip before he got in. Steam built like a wall around him as the water beat down, plastering his hair to his scalp and slicking away all remnants of the night.

Except his memories.

He could still see Jake kneeling before him, enveloping him in the wet heat of his mouth. Snarling, Cameron turned the water all the way to cold. The icy stream in no way reminded him of Troy's body pressed against him on the dance floor or the hot clasp of Jake's mouth on his dick.

His head began to clear, and by the time he shut off the water, he was shivering but thinking sanely. He rubbed himself dry, donned a pair of boxers, and flopped onto the bed.

He was pretty sure it wasn't cheating if a guy blew you while his boyfriend watched. Not that he'd ever been blown by a guy before, but the same principle applied as if it were a woman, right? Not that a woman had ever given him a blowjob while her boyfriend... He was off-topic.

Okay, not cheating. Next, was he bisexual?

Cameron stared at the smooth plaster of the ceiling. He'd been kind of thinking about this for a couple of days, and outright asking himself didn't disturb him as much as it had the first time. There was no denying that he was attracted—very attracted—to Jake and Troy. What they'd done at the club felt amazing. If that meant he was bisexual...

Huh. He really had reinvented himself. It felt good. It felt right.

So what now? Had leaving the nightclub so quickly, without talking to them, been cowardly? More to the point, did he wish he were back there?

His eyes drifted closed. If he'd stayed, what would have happened? Jake's dick had been hard as an iron spike when he kissed him. Maybe, instead of leaving, he could have unzipped Jake. He could have slid his hand inside and stroked the silk-over-steel shaft. Maybe he could have explored further and... what? He'd never touched a man there before. Except for himself. Was it the same?

He slipped his hand inside his boxers, over his half-hard cock. If he cupped Jake's balls, rolled them a little—like this—maybe squeezed gently, would Jake like it as much as Cameron did? Would Troy? A shudder overtook him.

And while he fondled Jake's sac, what would Troy do?

Cameron opened his eyes and got off the bed. What *would* Troy do?

five

"I PUSHED TOO HARD." Jake's voice, disembodied in the dark cocoon of their bed, was frustrated and unhappy.

"We," Troy corrected, taking his boyfriend's hand. "We pushed too hard." He sighed. "I really did think he was with us, though."

"Me, too." They lay in the hot, sticky darkness, and Troy listened to the soft sounds of the tropical night wafting through the open window. The sharp disappointment and hurt that had speared through him when Cameron fled still panged in his chest. He knew Jake felt the same, and worse, that Jake blamed himself.

Troy rolled toward Jake and propped himself up on an elbow. "You know I love you, right?"

The sheets rustled, and then the lamp went on. Troy blinked in the sudden light and squinted at his partner.

"What brought that on?" Jake was particularly hot in the middle of the night. Other people got bedhead and sleep creases. Not Jake. He got this sexy tousled thing, like in the movies. *What does Cam look like in the middle of the night?*

Troy dragged his attention back to the conversation. "I just want to make sure you know. I need you."

Jake smiled, his dimple popping out, and Troy put his pinkie finger in the dent, which made Jake laugh, like always.

Someone pounded on the front door.

Troy's hand fell back to the bed. "Who the hell...?" He and Jake both got up and put on shorts. Whoever it was kept pounding, so Troy picked up a cricket bat as well.

Jake flipped on the hall light as they approached the door. "Who is it?"

The pounding stopped. "It's Cameron."

Troy dropped the bat on his foot. "Son of a bitch!" His toes exploded with pain that radiated up over the top of his foot. He grabbed it and hopped awkwardly, tripping on the bat and falling shoulder-first into the wall. "Fuck!"

"What?" The slightly panicked sound to Cameron's voice wasn't quite drowned out by Jake's laughter as he unlocked the door. Cameron rushed in and stared at Troy. "What?"

"He's fine." Jake picked up the bat and propped it next to the door, where it couldn't do any more damage. Troy straightened, rubbing his shoulder, and tentatively put his foot on the floor. It throbbed, but the sharp edge was gone.

"I'm fine," he agreed. "Uh, come in." He gestured to the living room. Should he offer Cameron a drink? What the hell was the protocol when the man your boyfriend sucked off and who you'd hoped to have sex with came to your house in the middle of the night? He glanced at Jake behind Cameron's back and got a shrug in return. "Can we get you something?"

Cameron stood in front of the couch, gangly and awkward in his cargo shorts and T-shirt, and a surge of affection burst in Troy's chest. "No, I don't want anything. Well, that's not true. I do want something, but not to drink. What I mean—" He sighed and rubbed his eyes. "I suck at this."

Hope unfurled slowly. Troy cleared his throat. "I'm not usually too bad at it," he offered. "Why don't I start?"

Cameron hesitated, then nodded. "Okay. Well, let's sit down, first."

Cameron sat at one end of the couch. Jake had half-turned toward the armchair, but Troy recognized a good opportunity when it presented itself and dragged his boyfriend to sit at the other end of the couch, with himself in the middle.

"So," he began, angling his body toward Cameron and holding tightly to the strong warmth of Jake's hand. "I figure you're here because of what happened at the club."

Cameron exhaled a rush of air. "Yeah."

Troy nodded. "Great. I'll tell you where Jake and I are coming from. We've been together for six years, and this is it for both of us. We've never before thought about inviting a third person to our bed. Then we met you, and that changed."

"What Troy is trying to say diplomatically," Jake interrupted, "is that you make us both horny as hell."

Troy squeezed his hand. "Thanks, Jake. If you don't mind...?"

Jake shrugged, and Troy turned back to Cameron, who no longer looked like he was at his own funeral. "Anyway, I just want to make it clear that in the club, that wasn't just a spur of the moment thing. Well, it was, because we didn't plan it, but we were waiting for an opportunity to let you know how we felt. I get the feeling that we freaked you out a bit."

Cameron shook his head and sighed again. "No. I mean, yes, but not because... I thought I was straight, and..." He looked lost.

Beside Troy, Jake shifted. "Just because you enjoyed a blow job doesn't mean you're gay."

Cameron blinked and his expression re-animated. "But I'm pretty sure that wanting to play with your balls while Troy... Well, I still don't know what Troy would do, but I think it means I'm bi."

Troy's balls had become uncomfortably tight at the thought of Cameron playing with Jake's.

"I do have great balls."

Troy froze midbreath, but Cameron laughed, a sound of genuine happiness. A quick glance at Jake's face showed the dimple on display.

"I can't believe you just said that." Troy snatched his hand from Jake's grip.

Jake's smile turned from amused to predatory. "You have great balls, too. I love your balls. They're so soft and firm and they're the perfect size for me to take in my mouth and... suck."

Jake's gaze transfixed on Troy as he leaned in for a hot, needy kiss, the kind that had Troy's half-hard dick standing to full attention. He reached blindly behind him and grabbed on to Cameron—his leg, maybe. There was a long pause, filled only by the head-spinning sensation of Jake's mouth on his, and then Cameron's body pressed against Troy's back, and his arms reached around Troy to grab hold of Jake.

Jake broke their kiss and smiled his dark, sexy smile. "Hi."

Troy heard Cameron take a deep breath, and then he was pushed further into Jake as Cam leaned forward and met Jake's mouth with his own. Troy turned his head and nuzzled into the crook of Cam's neck, licking along his collarbone. Cameron pulled back, panting, and Jake extricated himself and stood.

He held out both hands. "Shall we?"

The bedroom was cool and dim, the only light coming from the streetlight outside the open window, filtering through tree branches. The bed was rumpled, and Cameron's gaze fixed on it.

More than anything, he wanted to be on that bed with Jake and Troy, but he was frozen, his feet glued to the floor.

A body nudged his from behind, and suddenly he was able to move. He turned, right into Troy's arms and a deep, soul-sucking kiss. Kissing a man was so different from kissing a woman. Where he was used to soft skin, there was the rough prickle of stubble. Where before there were smaller, slender bodies, now there were solid muscles and broad shoulders, perfect to hold on to. His eyelids drifted closed.

Hands kneaded his shoulders as Troy sucked on Cameron's tongue. Heat flooded his skin, and his dick pulsed in time with his heartbeat. He was guided backward, sandwiched between two hot, hard bodies, and then the one behind him—Jake—was gone and Cameron was lowered onto the mattress, Troy's mouth still glued to his.

Cameron opened his eyes as Troy drew back. Jake was propped on his side next to him, smiling his dark, sexy smile. As soon as Troy moved away, Jake swooped in, capturing Cameron's lips with his.

Jake's kisses were different from Troy's, harder, more demanding. His hands came down on Cameron's chest, tweaking his nipples through the thin fabric of his T-shirt. Tremors shook Cameron. He gasped brokenly into Jake's mouth, and then Jake pulled back and Troy was there again, naked this time. Jake climbed off the bed as Troy grasped the hem of Cameron's T-shirt, yanked it up over his head, and immediately went to work on the fastening of his shorts. Cameron pushed Troy's hands out of the way and did it himself, stripping naked in seconds.

Jake rejoined them on the bed, naked, and stroked his big, callused hands over Cameron's chest. Cameron shivered.

"Feels good, doesn't it?" Troy leaned over and captured one of Cameron's nipples between his teeth, the gentle scrape intensifying Cameron's shiver. Jake bit lightly on the flesh over Cameron's collarbone, then soothed the sting with his tongue.

"Do you trust us?" Jake's question hovered in the air for a long moment.

"Yes," Cameron finally answered and was rewarded with a long, addictive kiss from Troy.

"Okay, then. C'mere." Jake tugged Cameron up toward the head of the bed and pushed him back against the pillows while Troy rummaged through the nightstand drawer.

Seeing him withdraw condoms and lube, apprehension rose in Cameron, damping some of his lust. "Is it going to hurt?"

"If it does, we stop," Jake assured him. "You just have to

say. Okay?" Cameron nodded, and Jake grinned, his dimple flashing. Cameron's cock throbbed painfully.

"Just lie back and relax." Jake kissed him quickly, hard, and then kissed Troy. They were so sexy, both of them naked, their big, bronzed bodies shadowed in the dim room. He caught glimpses of their dicks, hard and straining, rubbing together, beautiful.

They broke apart, and Troy settled on his knees at the head of the bed while Jake moved to kneel between Cam's legs. Cameron watched through heavy-lidded eyes as Jake donned the condom. "Next time," Cameron whispered, shocking himself. "I want to do that."

Jake's gaze met his, and there was promise there. The lube was uncapped.

"Bend your knees," Troy told him. "And relax. Jake's an expert at this. He's gonna make you feel so good."

Cameron's balls tightened as he obeyed. Troy's slow drawl spoke of experience.

Jake swiped a thumb over the bead of cum welling from Cameron's dick. He lifted his hand to his lips and licked his thumb. "Mmm."

A shudder overtook Cameron.

Troy stroked a feather-light finger over Cameron's cheek, drawing his attention from Jake. "Ever sucked cock?" he whispered.

Cam's breath caught in his throat and excitement bloomed in his chest. He shook his head.

"Do you wanna?"

Cam nodded, eager beyond belief. He let Troy adjust the pillows, freezing at the first touch of Jake's lube-chilled fingers on his ass. No one had ever touched him there. It was scary, but his whole body was tense with excitement.

"Hey." Troy nudged his shoulder.

Cameron returned his attention to Troy, only to see a dick inches from his face. He swallowed, hard. He'd never seen a cock so close before. It was hard and pulsing, leaking a little at the tip. Impulsively, he licked the moisture away, his lips brushing the head. Troy shuddered and his dick bobbed. The taste of Troy's precum was different from what Cameron had expected. Salty and tangy and… good. He licked the head again, hovered for a moment, and then closed his lips over it.

Jake's finger slid into his ass, and he jerked, his teeth scraping Troy's dick. The sound Troy made was purely animalistic.

Jake paused. "Teeth? He likes it a bit rough."

Cameron focused on the thick finger in his ass. It felt… weird. Not bad, though. Then it moved, and shivers ran up and down his spine. That felt good. Really good. It was like every molecule in his body was focused on that one spot.

He turned his attention back to Troy's cock in his mouth. Running his tongue around the head as Jake gently stroked a finger in and out of his ass, he tried sucking lightly. Troy's hand slid into his hair and adjusted the position of Cam's head, allowing him to take more cock into his mouth. He tongued the underside, and Troy moaned.

Jake's finger was joined by another, and this time the inward slide burned. Not badly, but… Cameron squirmed on the impaling digits.

"Relax." Cameron's thigh muscles trembled at the rumble of Jake's deep voice, accompanied by the slight movement of his fingers.

Cameron's eyelids drifted closed, and he gave himself purely over to sensation. Jake's fingers in his ass. Troy's dick in his mouth. As Jake lightly moved his fingers, Cameron began to suck harder on Troy. He'd never done this before, but he knew what he liked himself. He trailed his hand over Troy's leg and hip until he found what he was looking for. Jake was right. Troy did have great balls. Cameron rolled them in his hand, loving the soft skin and the way Troy trembled in reaction.

Jake did something with his fingers, and Cameron moaned. Troy's echoing moan thrilled him. Jake's fingers withdrew, and Cam seized the moment. He relaxed his jaw and throat and took Troy as deep as he could. Troy's cock felt huge in his mouth. Remembering what Jake said, he lightly scraped his teeth over the tender flesh, squeezing Troy's balls at the same time.

Troy shouted and hot liquid splashed down Cam's throat. He swallowed desperately, eager not to miss a single drop of the thick tangy liquid, savoring each pulsing spurt, until Troy's grip in his hair eased and there were only a few drops left. Cam licked them away, and Troy withdrew. Cameron opened his eyes and met Troy's mouth with his. The kiss was tender, with none of the desperate need for release that Cameron was feeling.

Something hot and hard probed at the opening of Cameron's ass, and he stiffened. Troy broke their kiss. "Shh. Just relax and push out."

Cameron sucked in a deep breath and tried to relax his muscles. He lifted his head and his gaze met Jake's. The other man was sweating, his face tight. Cameron wanted to writhe under the pressure of Jake's dick as he inched into his ass. The head was sucked in, and there was a slow, burning slide. Jake's cock was so much thicker than his fingers, stretched Cameron so much more, and he didn't know if he liked it or not. Then Jake withdrew to the tip and a broken cry burst from Cameron.

A hand closed around Cameron's cock, and he tore his

gaze away from Jake's cock sliding in and out of his ass to watch Troy stroke him. Jake pressed back in as Troy's hand glided down Cameron's shaft. The two of them acted in rhythm, stroking in and out, up and down, faster and faster, while Cameron's balls ached and his muscles quivered. The tingles began at the base of his spine, building and building until the pressure was unbearable, and then he came in long, glorious, relief-pulsing spurts, his cum spraying over Troy and Jake.

Troy crawled back up and kissed him, a deep, drugging kiss, while Jake thrust harder, deeper, and then groaned, a sound so erotic that Cameron's dick stirred again.

six

CAMERON HELPED the teenager with his flippers, then stood back so the boy could get to the water. It was so cool, seeing kids experience the reef for the first time.

The three months he'd been in Cairns had been the best of his life. After that first night with Jake and Troy, he'd moved out of the hotel and into their house and never looked back.

He'd long since gotten his dive certificate, and at Jake's suggestion now helped out on the cruises. It gave him the chance to dive for free and to spend time with Jake and Troy. They'd even organized some days when all three of them were off work so they could go sightseeing together.

Now his vacation was nearly over. In three days, he was due to fly back to the States. He didn't want to go. He'd come to Australia to reinvent himself, and it had worked. He wasn't Cameron-the-geek anymore.

Cam glanced down at his Sail Away uniform and tanned arms and legs. He was this person now, not the office drone from New York. He shuddered at the thought of being cooped up indoors all day.

Troy's laugh caught his attention. The beginner dive group was getting ready to go in, and Cam watched for a moment as Troy helped a middle-aged woman adjust her oxygen tank. Troy and Jake were the best thing that had ever happened to him, and leaving them would break his heart.

But he couldn't stay. Eventually, they'd want to go back to their normal lives and normal relationship, and then he'd be alone, observing from the outside. Jobless, home-less, and alone.

He had to go back.

Troy leaned his forehead against the cool surface of the filing cabinet. His head pounded, a painful rhythm due entirely to stress.

A hand closed over his nape and squeezed, easing into a gentle massage. Troy straightened and turned into Jake's arms.

"He's going to leave." His words were muffled by Jake's shoulder.

Jake's arms tightened around Troy. "I know."

Troy pulled back. "Can't we do something?"

Jake let him go and turned away, running a hand over his head. "We knew he'd leave eventually. If he wanted to stay, he would."

Cam was still on board the boat, helping the crew lock it down for the night. Troy had hurried back to the office after making a stupid excuse, desperate for the comfort of Jake's arms.

Troy propped himself on the edge of the desk. "Surely you don't think we were just a holiday fling for him?"

Jake shrugged, gaze steadfastly focused through the door into the front room of the office. "Has he ever said anything to make us think otherwise?"

Troy opened his mouth, a hot rebuttal on the tip of his tongue, then closed it again. Jake was right. Cam was affectionate, passionate, and always seemed happy to be with them, but he'd never once said anything about wanting to *stay* with them.

"He belongs here." Troy heard the whiny tone to his voice but couldn't help it. "He can't go back to his stupid job doing whatever he did. He should be a dive instructor. He'd be great at it; you've seen how he is with the beginners. And he could buy into the business."

"I know." Jake sighed and sat next to Troy. "But if he wanted to do that, wouldn't he have said?" He drummed his fingers on the desk, beside his leg. "We could offer."

Troy shook his head, vehemently. "No. If he doesn't want to, it might make him feel awkward. I don't want him to move out early. I want these last few days with him."

"Okay." Jake took Troy's hand and squeezed. "So we ask him right before he leaves."

Troy squeezed back.

Let's take the boat out. Troy's suggestion had seemed casual enough. One last dive before he left tomorrow night. They'd taken the boat out to the pontoon, timing it so they arrived just after the tourist boat left. That gave them nearly three hours of daylight for a leisurely dive before heading home in the balmy evening.

Except now, after their dive, they were raiding the

pontoon kitchen and their conversation was so stilted they'd long since fallen into silence.

"So…" Cam jumped at the sound of Jake's voice. "Do you have plans for when you get back to New York?"

Cam shrugged. "I go back to work next week," he mumbled. "I guess I'll go grocery shopping or something."

"Isn't it cold in New York now?" Troy's voice had an edge to it that Cam hadn't heard before.

"Yes." Cam fiddled with the band of his watch, a waterproof dive watch he'd bought when he'd started spending so much time underwater. He couldn't look at Jake and Troy, couldn't bear to see their faces. He'd break down and beg.

"Fuck this." A hand grabbed his arm in a vise-like grip and yanked him out of his seat. He jerked his head up to see the determined expression on Jake's face. "Come on, Troy."

A moment later, Troy fell into step beside them. "Where?" he asked.

"Observatory." Jake's tone was clipped.

"What are you doing? Guys, we should be getting back." Cam's protest seemed to piss off Jake, if the white line around his mouth was any indication. A tiny flame of hope kindled in his chest.

Jake hustled him across the pontoon and then down the stairs to the observatory, Troy preceding them.

"Okay, here's the thing." Jake finally let Cam go. "We've grown very attached to you, and we're going to miss you way too much."

"I—" Cam's voice caught in his throat. "I'm going to miss you too."

He launched himself at Jake, wrapping his arms around him and slamming his mouth against Jake's. Seconds later, he felt Troy's body press against his back and Troy's mouth nuzzle the sensitive skin behind his ear. Jake's tongue delved into his mouth and dueled with his. Cam closed his eyes and gave himself over to the wonderful, dizzying sensations. Jake pulled back and Cam protested wordlessly.

"Turn," Jake ordered. His tone thrilled Cam—the dark, possessive sound was always a precursor to an incredible fuck.

Cam turned. Troy smiled at him and crouched down. "Lean forward and brace your hands on the window."

Cam obeyed. Troy was stroking Cam's crotch, unfastening his shorts, and Cam could hear the rustle of Jake's clothes behind him. Cam's jeans were lowered, and the tension in the air ratcheted up. His stomach flipped excitedly.

Troy's breath whispered over Cam's dick, and then hot, wet heaven engulfed him. Jake smoothed a hand down Cam's back and into the cleft between his cheeks. A finger rimmed his ass, and Cam shuddered. Jake chuckled, and another finger joined the first, this one cold and wet. Lube?

He heard the crackle of a condom packet, but then Troy's tongue dipped into the slit of Cam's cockhead, and Cam groaned. He leaned into Troy's mouth, putting his weight onto his hands as Jake pressed his cock in that first aching inch.

Troy swallowed, the movement massaging, and Jake thrust deep. Cam threw his head back, desperately sucking in air as spine-tingling electricity pulsed through him, but they'd stopped.

"Wha—?" Why didn't they move? Jake was in him, Troy's mouth paradise around him, but they were still when he wanted them to move.

"Stay with us." Jake's whisper cut through Cam's agonized introspection. "Promise you'll stay."

Cam's heart leapt. Did they mean...? No, it was just the sex. "Yes," he mumbled around the lump in his throat.

"Promise." Jake insisted, shifting fractionally, the movement sending shockwaves careening through Cam.

A moan was torn from his throat. "I promise."

As if a switch had been flipped, Troy's mouth moved, his tongue sliding over Cam's shaft while Jake withdrew from his ass and then rammed back in.

Within seconds, he was spiraling out of control. He couldn't hold on, not with Troy's mouth and Jake's powerful thrusts. His balls drew up, and he came, his cry of satisfaction echoing through the observatory.

Jake wrapped the condom in a tissue and tossed it in the trashcan under the staircase, then zipped his shorts. Triumph thundered through him.

"So..." Cameron sounded awkward, and Jake noticed his hand shook as he fastened his own shorts. "Um. That was —really great. Thanks. We should get back. I'm not finished packing."

The blood rushed from Jake's head, and he swayed.

What the fuck?

"What are you talking about?" Troy grabbed Cam's arm. "You said you were going to stay with us. You *promised*." There was no mistaking his accusatory tone.

"I—" Cam met Jake's gaze, and Jake saw the emotion welling in his eyes. "You meant that?"

"Of course we did!" Troy burst out, squeezing Cam's

hand. "Did you think we just wanted one last fuck? We were trying to convince you to stay."

Cam took a deep breath, then another. "I—I want to stay." His voice was so low, Jake leaned forward to catch the words.

"This is how it's going to be." Jake kept his tone businesslike. Until everything was spelled out, he couldn't get his hopes up. Not like earlier. "You'll stay here. With us. We love you. If you want, you can be a dive instructor. And when you're ready, you can buy into the company, so we'll all be equal partners. But the most important thing is, *you're staying.*"

Cam gazed down at where Troy's hand gripped his and then back up at Jake, who struggled not to break down and beg.

"I'm staying." A smile bloomed across Cam's face. "I love you. I love you both so much, I don't know how I lived before you."

Jake took Cam's and Troy's free hands and lifted them to his lips. Time to go home.

Cam held on to Jake's hand as Troy steered the boat back toward Cairns. The night air swept across his skin, the salt spray blowing in his face. Behind him, Troy made a comment about dinner, and Jake responded.

Forget being reinvented. He knew exactly who he was.

And now he was home.

Thanks for reading about my Aussie boys!

We talk spoilers in my Facebook reader group, RoMMance
with Becca & Louisa.
Or you can subscribe to my newsletter to get all updates
and access to bonus scenes: https://bit.ly/LouisaMBonus.

For early access to chapters of my upcoming books,
artwork, and other bonus material, check out my Patreon
here: patreon.com/louisamasters

also by louisa masters

Saddles & Suits

Alistair's Extraordinaries

Grave Situation

Elemental Men: The Complete Series

Style Me

Rebrand

Couture

Elf Magic

Wooing the Wiccan

Enticing the Elf

The Collective

Higher Demon

Demon Hunter

Demons-In-Law

Asher

Micah

Zachary

Franklin U

Mr. Romance

The Holigay Hookup *related novella

Batting Style

Ghostly Guardians

Spirited Situation

Vortex Conundrum

Conduit Crisis

Gateway Catastrophe

Here Be Dragons

Dragon Ever After

The Professor's Dragon

The Dragon Experiment

Conspiracy of Dragons

Hidden Species

Demons Do It Better

One Bite With A Vampire

Hijinks With A Hellhound

Sorcerers Always Satisfy

Hidden Species Box Set

Met His Match

Charming Him

Offside Rules

A Christmas Chance (novella)

Between the Covers (M/F)

Joy Universe

I've Got This

Follow My Lead

In Your Hands

<u>Take Us There</u>

Novellas

Fake It 'Til You Make It (permafree)

One Golden Night

O Hell, All Ye Shoppers

Out of the Office

After the Blaze

Blokes Down Under Novella Collection

Louisa Masters started reading romance much earlier than her mother thought she should. As an adult, she feeds her addiction in every spare second. She spent years trying to build a "sensible" career, working in bookstores, recruitment, resource management, administration, and as a travel agent before finally conceding defeat and devoting herself to the world of romance novels.

Louisa has a long list of places first discovered in books that she wants to visit, and every so often she overcomes her loathing of jet lag and takes a trip that charges her imagination. She lives in Melbourne, Australia, where she whines about the weather for most of the year while secretly admitting she'll probably never move.

http://www.louisamasters.com

www.ingramcontent.com/pod-product-compliance
Lightning Source LLC
Chambersburg PA
CBHW032101050726

47590CB00001B/364